CW01582349

Praise for book one in the series, *About Last Summer*:

"Marina Magdalena has crafted an intriguing story that explores the ranging emotions of teen-hood with the pressures teenagers feel in this world. She has a great understanding of the teenage mind and emotions, and expresses them in a heart-wrenching story that is beautifully crafted.

About Last Summer is a brilliant book that will open conversations between parents and kids in a wonderfully healing way."

Becs Millington, radio presenter at UCB

"In her debut novel, Marina Magdalena takes young readers on an exciting, laugh-out-loud journey – with enough dark twists and drama to keep them fully engaged to the very end.

About Last Summer introduces us to the inner world of young teen Antigone Kingsley. She is both complex and relatable, and demonstrates many aspects of what it means to be human. It is a heart-warming but hilarious story of redemption, and a lesson in feeling the fear and doing it anyway.

With unlikely heroes and gripping cliff-hangers, this book certainly leaves the reader wanting to see what's next for Antigone and her friends."

Emma-Jayne Browne, play therapist and psychotherapist

"A story skilfully told, written with warmth and heart, *Antigone Kingsley: About Last Summer* explores the tumultuous world of a teenager struggling to recognise her own self-worth. It's a story of friendship, jealousy, tragedy, forgiveness, and redemption, set against the evocative backdrop of a struggling theatre.

Marina Magdalena captures the voice of a young teen perfectly, taking us on a roller coaster of emotion. This book is a page-turner that tackles timeless themes with a fresh, contemporary voice. It had me gripped until the last page."
Daniel Ingram-Brown, author

"*About Last Summer* encompasses family life, catastrophes, and the pain of teenage years through perceptive writing, born from a deep understanding of teen emotions and behaviour.

It is insightful and beautifully written by one who truly understands the teenage journey and all the emotions along the way. I was drawn in to Tig's mind and felt her confusion, disappointment, and anger . . . and ultimately her decision to take responsibility for her actions. I cared deeply for her, even as she raged against her situation and made mistakes – then I rejoiced as she reflected, understood, and matured.

This engaging first novel reflects the complications of family life, the shock reactions to sudden change, and the challenges of navigating a confusing and complicated world. It has an underlying wisdom that will resonate with those reading it, whatever their age."
Kay Benbow, children's media specialist

Young people's reviews of *About Last Summer*:

"I loved *About Last Summer*. It is gripping and such a heartwarming story, with relatable teenage emotions and

brilliantly written. It has got to be one of my most-loved books."
Alexia-Carolina, 13

"I love Tig. We could be friends; I find her character is so relatable. We'd get up to lots of ADHD mischief together!"
Silver, 11

"I love *About Last Summer*. It has a gripping storyline, and I feel like I know Tig personally. Whenever I read it, I can't help but laugh."
Freya, 12

"I really loved Tig. Her story is fun and relatable in so many ways! I think this is such a good book for a teen who just needs a laugh. I cannot wait for book two!"
Willa, 12

"This is my favourite book! I LOVE Tig, she is really funny. She always tries her best and she is very relatable."
Leonie, 11

"Tig makes me laugh so much and I adore her friendship with Fidge. This book is so heartwarming to read."
Amara, 12

"*About Last Summer* was an exciting read and kept me on the edge of my seat! I love the bond between Fidge and Tig."
Amani, 15

ANTIGONE KINGSLEY

DON'T JUDGE ME

BY MARINA MAGDALENA

First published in Great Britain in 2024

Marylebone House
Studio 101, The Record Hall,
16–16A Baldwins Gardens,
London, EC1N 7RJ
www.marylebonehousebooks.co.uk

Copyright © Marina Magdalena 2024

All rights reserved. No part of this book may be reproduced or transmitted in any form or by any means, electronic or mechanical, including photocopying, recording, or by any information storage and retrieval system, without permission in writing from the publisher.

This is a work of fiction and, except in the case of historical fact, any resemblance to actual persons, living or dead, is purely coincidental.

British Library Cataloguing-in-Publication Data
A catalogue record for this book is available from the British Library

ISBN 978-1-910674-72-7
eBook ISBN 978-1-910674-73-4

Typeset by Fakenham Prepress Solutions, Fakenham, Norfolk NR21 8NL
First printed in Great Britain by Clays

eBook by Fakenham Prepress Solutions, Fakenham, Norfolk NR21 8NL

Produced on paper from sustainable forests

For Mum and Dad

Introduction

Hey, brand-new, fresh-paged, sparkly clean notebook . . .

It's me – Tig! Before you freak out, this is not *another confession, and nothing terrible has happened – well, not yet anyway. I am one week away from a full-on Switzerland adventure and I thought: hey, if last year I could fill a notebook about my dangerously insane summer where I very nearly landed myself in a high-security prison for the attempted murder of my perfect French cousin Amelie, then why not have one dedicated to the good stuff too?*

A lot *has happened since I last checked in. I still live above the Nicostrata Theatre, which, guess what, is still open. I know, right, even though we skimmed the edge of financial disaster (not helped by me and my big sis Ismene driving away our only paying lodger), my parents have been modernizing their usual Greek tragedy vibes with more relatable plays that the good folk of Brinstock actually* want *to come and watch. And since my initial wobbly start of combining my YouTube channel with the Old Nic, things have picked up online, which means all the best shows want to perform on our dusty old stage. It's crazy what some viral hype can do!*

Oh, and my channel, JustTigging, is thriving too. Remember how I livestreamed my accidental sabotage of Amelie's aerial silk performance to the whole world – the moment I nearly, accidentally, attemptedly murdered her? And how about twenty thousand people saw my thirteen-year-old cousin fall to the floor like a rag doll? Well, my followers forgot about it a lot quicker than I did! So now I am back to my usual pranks on the unsuspecting public, but with a bit more sophistication rolled into it. I am fourteen in a few months and Ismene is fifteen already, so we have tried to add some intelligent "Hey guys, let me tell you all about my day . . ." to the dressing up, special-effects make-up and slapstick comedy. I am trying to create an "I'm still good old Tig" image (just a little older, wiser and less manic). It is going well. I even managed to straighten my hair once. Just once, though, because I scolded my fingers, my arms ached so bad I wanted to cry and then I forgot to unplug the straighteners and nearly set fire to our home.

But hey, for at least two videos and a short reel I didn't have a mass of frizzy brown hair. You see, I am growing!

What else . . .? Fidge! I love him SO. MUCH. I mean, not love love him, not like that. We are not dating. I am still thirteen, remember! What I mean is, I hurt a lot of people last summer, emotionally, physically . . . maybe mentally scarred a few. I definitely scarred our ex-lodger Marcus when I convinced him in a prank that he was the cursed ghost of a despicable Roman soldier – some say he still mutters to himself about his former disgraced life – so that is at least one person. Over the last nine months I have had to show people they can trust me. I don't go as crazy as I used to. I don't laugh as loud. I don't leave everything to the last minute. I don't let myself stand out too much. As far as most people in school and our little old town of Brinstock know, Antigone Kingsley, the loud, hyperactive and slightly bonkers girl of last summer, has gone away. I am like a butterfly stepping out from my foolish caterpillar ways, like the duckling becoming a swan or the . . . okay, you get the idea. The point is, outside of my family everyone totally buys into the new me and it is really working. But on those weekends with Fidge, when we hang out on our skateboards and plan fun new pranks, when we race down the grassy banks at the back of his house until our feet give way and we end up flying–falling to the bottom at full speed . . . on those weekends I get to be Tig. That makes Fidge my favourite human on the planet.

Anyway, like I said, one week until my Switzerland adventure and I am ready! *I have picked out some Ismene- and Amelie-approved clothes, curated a playlist that keeps me feeling chilled, given the heads-up to my followers that things are going continental, and even bought myself a new notebook. You see – life is* good. *I am not worried about spending time away from home with no parents in a completely unknown country. I know last summer was horrible, but that was last summer. This is spring, a fresh start for the new and improved Antigone Kingsley. I am* good. *NOTHING is going to go wrong!*

Okay, good . . . deep breaths . . . I can do this.

PART ONE

One

". . . which is how upthrust works. It isn't really about the plane flying; it is about it falling but not crashing . . . Fascinating, really . . ."

Dad had been talking non-stop since the plane left the runway. I'm not sure if he was giving me a physics lesson or if deep down he was a nervous flyer attempting to soothe himself with science. Either way he showed no signs of stopping.

"To think the human mind capable of conceiving flight . . ."

His voice seeped into the hum of the engine. I felt restless. I checked my watch and saw that we had only been in the air for thirty minutes. Thirty very boring minutes. I shuffled up in my seat to see if I could spot my big sis Ismene, but the giant snoring dude sat next to me had wedged me in like a slice of ham slapped between two chunks of tasteless, boring bread.

My dad was still hypothesizing: "If man, or a woman of course, can *fly metal* into space, then what's to say we can't take it to the middle of the earth? How far have we *actually* drilled down?"

One

Panic wrapped itself around me like an oversized coat and I fought the rising urge to flap my hands in the air and scream at these men to give me some space. I tried to settle my vision on the chair in front of me, but it felt far too close! I leaned forward into the brace position and closed my eyes. I took long deep breaths. *I'm in an open field surrounded by a cloudless sky above me, a blanket of grass beneath me and oxygen, beautiful clean oxygen . . . Breathe, Antigone, you're nearly there . . .*

I was chilling in my imaginary bed of flowers for no more than three seconds when Snoring Guy yawned and shuffled in his seat. The sound of his teeth grinding pulled me abruptly back to reality. I shifted my body closer to the seat in front. If I could walk through chairs I would be in the cockpit telling the pilot to stick some throttle on and speed things up. Snoring Guy's sleeping brain detected the empty space behind me and snatched the opportunity, spreading out his arms and allowing his elbow to lollop onto my seat. Nice one! Now I would have to sit with my nose pressed against the chair all flight.

I looked over at Dad, willing him to do something about the hot air and the no space and the way the seconds seemed to move really, really slowly. But he was not getting any of my silent pleading. He was too busy pondering.

"I imagine a few hundred years from now the discovery of new technologies . . ." Dad was caught on a loop. He was never going to rescue me from this horrible, shrinking space. Boring I can handle, but trapped between Snoring Guy's lolloping shoulder, Dad the scientist and piles of bags, it became too much.

I threw my arms in front of me, preserving what little space I had left, and said in my firmest voice, "Out! I need to get out! You need to move, please!"

My dad spluttered back to reality. "Everything okay, Tig?"

"It's fine. I just need to get out, please." I was standing as best as I could between two rows of chairs, a carpet of bags and a dropped ceiling. I knew Snoring Guy could hear me; his breathing had sped up and his face looked less droopy than a moment before.

"Can you please move, sir?"

He tightened his eyes a little more as Dad tried to softly wake him. "Excuse me, fella. My daughter just needs to . . ."

I couldn't wait any longer. The guy was being awkward. I pushed myself forward, ramming my knees against his and deliberately standing on his toes while stating loudly, "Sorry, coming through . . . Oops, if I can get . . . Oh, thanks." In the corner of my eye, I watched Snoring Guy wince in discomfort as my feet rolled across his shoes. He shuffled just enough for me to thrust myself into the aisle. I was free, but only for a moment. I looked up the aircraft and saw a trolley on its way towards me. I looked behind me and saw a woman battling up the aisle with a wriggling toddler in her arms. With no time to lose, I pushed myself through the movement of people and straight to the empty seat next to Mum and Ismene. I landed haphazardly in the seat, closed my eyes and took three deep breaths. The air felt freer here.

Mum pulled her eyes away from her book. "I thought you wanted to keep Dad company?"

I considered telling the truth, but then a better idea sprang to mind. "Dad is coming up with these amazing ideas."

"Really!?" Mum loves ideas like I love wide open spaces and room to stretch.

"I thought you might be interested to hear them, I mean, it's really facilitating stuff! So anyway, I came to get you while he is still in the flow." Mum also loves "flow" like I loved the empty seat next to hers.

"Great! Thanks, Tiggy, that's very thoughtful." Mum sprang to her feet, her tiny frame slipping through the chairs like a delicate fairy, before bouncing towards the love of her life.

Space. Beautiful space. The air felt cooler and quieter down this end. I danced my feet in little circles, enjoying the lack of bags in my way.

Ismene was smiling at me. "What fascinating ideas is Dad coming up with?" There was a hint of sarcasm in her voice.

I chuckled at the thought of Mum sitting through his monologue about drilling to middle earth. "Something about technology and the incredible potential of humans in science." Ismene's eyes skipped a little with excitement and I remembered that this was her kind of conversation. I also remembered that this was exactly why she should be keeping Dad company instead of me. I changed the subject before Ismene had a chance to keep it going. "Where are the snacks?"

My sister's smile lit up even brighter. We both knew she had been planning travel snacks for the last three weeks. Ismene is the kind of person who likes to plan everything. I used to think it was because she was scared about forgetting something or hated the idea of failing due to poor preparation, but over the last few years I have come to realize that she just can't help herself. Planning is not a line of defence for Ismene; it's a way of life. Need something to do at the weekend? Ismene's got a solution for that. Lost your school project? She has you covered. Found yourself trapped in the middle of an alien invasion? Yep, she has got a plan for that too.

Ismene hauled her bag out of the footwell and onto her lap before pouring a multitude of sweet and salty treats onto the tray. She began organizing the treats into piles and, knowing she would be there for a while, I seized the opportunity for peace, popped my headphones onto my head and took a few deep breaths. The outside world faded away as warm, pulsing music floated into my mind. It was all good. There was nothing to worry about, and yet . . .

I tried to keep my mind positive, but the same nagging little thought grabbed my attention: I had to get to Paris, spend the night with my cousin and her parents, fly to Switzerland, just me and two other teenagers, make our way to Alpine Adventure Youth Camp – and do it *all* without any adults, without accidentally annoying Amelie, without forgetting all my things or getting lost and ending up in some other country. This was going to be a disaster!

I turned the music up to drown out my own negativity, but there was a tapping on my hand. I opened my eyes and Ismene poured a pile of snacks onto my tray. I wasn't hungry, but I picked up a pretzel anyway and tucked in.

Issy focused all of her attention on me. "We're landing soon. Are you okay?" I nodded emphatically and she kept going. "When you see Amelie, try to be casual. Act like you have always been friends."

I pretended I didn't know what she was talking about. "We *are* friends!"

She ignored my blank denial and kept pushing. "Don't bring up last summer, not even as a joke. Just forget that was a *thing* . . ."

"I know!" I rolled my eyes and pretended I wasn't bothered about anything, but it wasn't true. Ever since my mum and Auntie Kate had arranged for us to go to Alpine Adventure Youth Camp, I had been reliving the moment I almost murdered my cousin Amelie, over and over again. Not just the accident, and it *was* an accident, by the way, but the hospital visit, the police station, the arguments with Fidge – all of it. And my family had been acting really weird with me too. They kept pretending they weren't thinking about my dark side, always speaking positively in over-enthusiastic voices, but I saw them giving me the side-eye. They were waiting for me to do something crazy and unpredictable.

I suddenly realized that Issy was still talking at me. ". . . but you can still wear your jeans."

I had no idea what she was saying – I'd stopped listening when she mentioned last summer. I could see her waiting for a reply. "Okay, got it!"

She smiled at me, but her glittery blue eyes were scouring my face, trying to work out if I'd heard anything she just said.

I tried to ease her concerns: "Issy, you don't need to worry about me and Amelie. We have been chatting for the last nine months and we haven't argued once."

My sister jumped in with, "But what if you feel left out again?"

"I promise if I feel left out I'll come and talk to you instead of nearly killing our cousin!" I flashed her a quick smile and she seemed to accept it.

I was so done with these conversations! I felt like a dangerous animal that everyone was trying to keep calm. The only person who didn't seem to be nervous about our Alpine adventure was Fidge, mainly because he always thinks everything is going to be amazing, but he also knows better than to add more drama to my drama. Sadly, I wouldn't be seeing him for another three long weeks. I switched on my phone and tapped on his messages. It was on flight mode, so there was nothing new, but I reread our last conversation.

FIDGE: [A selfie of him and my fat, fluffy, ginger fur ball of a cat, Taco]
I fed him his breakfast. He had lasagne.

ME:	Funny! You have to stay with him for a while so he doesn't feel lonely
FIDGE:	I will be here ages. I am reading another one of your notebooks . . .
	[I ignore the joke, but he knows I'm laughing]
ME:	You can tidy my room while you are there
FIDGE:	When do you take off?
ME:	Now. See you on the other side

I could feel my whole body relax into my seat as I remembered Fidge reading through my notebook all about last summer. He'd read the whole confession in one day and I sat and watched him. I was terrified of him reading it and hating me, especially the parts about our fight. But he laughed through most of the pages and then blushed occasionally (that was awkward). He didn't seem that bothered about my meltdowns or my hatred towards Amelie. I know he was there and saw the whole thing, but what people see of me and the thoughts in my head can be two very different things. I'd squirmed with embarrassment for at least the first ten pages, but after a while I actually felt relieved. It is surprisingly nice to have someone know all about you and still like you. Especially someone like Fidge. Once he had finished the final page, he stood up, gave me a high-five and we went and got some pizza.

I clicked on to his profile picture. He had changed the selfie of us on skateboards to one of him and Taco. His big brown eyes smiled through a mass of chocolate-brown wavy hair. It was only April, but his skin was already dark and summery against Taco's ginger and white fluff. Taco looked unimpressed.

The captain interrupted my reminiscing with an announcement: "Cabin crew, ten minutes. Prepare the cabin for landing."

A flurry of movement swept through the plane as tray tables were secured and seatbelts clicked on. Ismene began to gather all the remaining snacks and poured them carefully into her bag. Even with her long hair falling over her face I could still feel her excitement. She couldn't wait to see Amelie.

I took a deep breath and reminded myself that everything would be all right. This was *not* going to be a disaster! Amelie liked me now . . . It had all been a stupid misunderstanding. We were friends. We were *cousins*! Everything was going to be *fine*!

Two

I was so pre-occupied with the sheer weight and bulk of my luggage that I barely noticed walking into the arrivals lounge in Paris. It had only been just over an hour's flight from London but long enough for me to over-think the pros and cons of the next few weeks. My heart was a jittery mess of excitement and nerves as the bustling crowds of travellers filled the terminal with energy and expectation. I navigated through the sea of faces, desperately trying to keep up with my family, who were either insanely strong or didn't pack half as much as me. I thought of the random camera equipment, costumes and SFX make-up that I had thrust into my suitcase at the last minute, and I instantly regretted bringing so much stuff. I found a clearing by the huge glass doors and stopped in the hope that someone from my family would come and find me.

The last time I'd been at an airport was to collect Amelie and take her back to our home for the summer. The thought sent a shiver darting down my back as I remembered her in that white dress, her blonde luscious locks bouncing around her face like a halo and the whole world stopping to gaze at her. I looked down at my bright pink sweater and wondered why I'd thought that was the best outfit to travel in.

Just then, Mum poked her head through the glass doors. "Come on, Tiggy. Dad is collecting us a car."

I grabbed hold of my luggage and trudged clunkily after my mum, who was in full organizer mode. She moved easily between the crowds and led us to the car, where my dad and Ismene were already waiting. Issy was snuggled into her seat, surrounded by sweaters, bags and her phone – always on her phone! I couldn't resist the opportunity to interrupt her peace a little. I swung open the car door she had been resting her elbow on and climbed in on top of her, pretending I had no idea she was there. I squashed myself into her body, gently but deliberately taking up as much space as I could while pressing her head against the car seat.

She yelled out at me, "No, Tiiiiiig! Use the other door!" But I could hear from her giggles that she found it hilarious.

Still on her lap, I pretended to make myself comfortable for the drive, resting my head on her face. She laughed some more. In the front seats, Dad was drumming his hands frustratedly against the steering wheel and Mum was checking the route to Amelie's house on her phone. Sensing Dad's impatience, Mum tried a bit of half-hearted chiding: "Girls . . . settle down, please!" But she was too engrossed in her map to put any energy into it. I did one final squish before rolling into the middle seat, half taking my sister with me. Her laughs turned to huffs as she caught a glimpse of her hair in the mirror and began putting everything back into place.

My eyes scanned the airport building, the rows of cars and hurried people as I settled into my seat. It was gloomy outside, but if I got really close to the glass and looked up, I could just about catch a glimpse of sunshine squeezing through the clouds. I opened the car window a little and took in the smell of old rainwater. Leftover puddles gathered in the dips in the road, waiting to be trampled by small children, heavy boots and high stiletto heels. From every direction, cars were stop-starting, pulling in and out of spaces and trying to navigate the illusive route out of the airport.

I slid on my headphones and pressed play on my favourite queen of pop. The music rolled over me like a fleece blanket as I snuggled into my seat, singing silently to the lyrics in my head and feeling my body dance under my skin without even moving.

My dad drove cautiously out of the airport, his hands clutching the steering wheel as though he was expecting the car to run away. The engine rumbled quietly beneath the music while Mum cooed over Paris. "Kevin, look, that's new!"

Inside the car, it was toasty and warm. I nestled my thoughts deeper into my headphones as music whirled around my brain like a sparkly puff of happiness as I leaned into melody and lyrics.

In the distance I could hear Dad stressing out over the directions. "Laura, you can't tell me once we're sat at the traffic lights – I have no idea where I'm going. Put the phone where I can see it."

Mum was still moving the phone around and I could see the map rotating on the screen, desperately trying to figure out whether these middle-aged folk wanted to view the map in portrait or landscape. I pictured myself showing them, for the one hundredth time, how to lock the screen, but it felt like too much effort.

Tiredness seeped in. I had no interest in traffic or Paris or joining Ismene, who was probably messaging Amelie.

My eyes felt heavy . . .

My breathing slowed as my eyelids dropped closed. I could feel my body slumping into a deep sleep, but my imagination was only just getting started.

Songs weave in and out of each other as shifting rhythms and blending melodies bring new glows racing and swirling into my mind. I'm floating, then falling, then running, jumping, back to floating. I am in my happy place, completely still on the outside but dancing effortlessly through one song to the next to the next. I am lost in a haze of sweet imagination when . . .

Suddenly my neck fell forward and my head darted to attention.

"Ah! You are 'ere!" The car door opened and a rush of cool air raced up my body. We couldn't be at Amelie's house already? "Leave your bags. We can get zem later. Come in, come in!"

That thick Parisian accent could mean only one thing: Uncle Jacques. We really were here!

I blinked my eyes and stretched my arms wide, readjusting my senses to the real world. My parents were flapping in the front of the car, manoeuvring bags and keys and bizarrely a giant paper map of Paris. Maybe I *should* have locked their phone screen on landscape . . . Ismene's door was open and her seat was empty. My eyes traced along the route from her car seat and up the pathway until they landed on my sister, arms flung around my cousin as they bounced in an excited cuddle.

A bubble of energy exploded inside me, waking me up and thrusting me out of the car. I ran towards Amelie, both of us squealing inaudible things about being super-happy to see each other before folding into a big warm hug. Not the old "I hate you, Tig" reluctant hug, but the kind she usually kept just for my sister. I tightened my arms around her and nestled my face in her long blonde hair.

"I am so happy you are here!" my cousin whispered into my ear.

"Me too," I replied. Our hug slipped into a girl huddle, joined eagerly by Issy. We walked, the three of us, arm in arm up the long driveway and into Amelie's house.

"You have to come and see my room. I have filled it with snacks, and I thought we could watch a movie and have a sleepover . . ." Amelie's voice smudged into the background as I took in her elegant home as though it was all new. We had been visiting Amelie's my whole life, but for the first time since I could remember it actually felt pretty good to be there!

Three

Me: What you doing?
Fidge: Playing with your cat.
Me: Taco doesn't like to play.
Fidge: He does with me.
We are bonding.
How's Paris?
Me: Good.
I am with Amelie.
Her room is amazing.

"Tig, you're going to love this!"

I snapped out of my phone daze to see Amelie and Issy engrossed in something on the laptop. I slipped my phone back into my pocket and scrambled across the floor to see what they were looking at.

"Alpine Adventure Youth Camp." I heard myself saying the words out loud and at once bubbles of happy anticipation started to float gently through my body. A whole fourteen days away from our home, adventuring in the mountains of Switzerland! Admittedly the thought had terrified me when Dad announced it to us a few months before, but seeing the deep green mountains, the sparkly lake and blue cloudless sky, it felt like a ticket to heaven (but obviously not with the dying bit).

Amelie kept flicking through images on the website and a little squeal of excitement escaped my lips. “Amelie, I can’t believe your parents have paid for us to go too!”

A quick image of Auntie Kate standing over Amelie’s hospital bed and telling us that we would *never* see Amelie for the rest of our lives (or something like that) popped into my head like a movie, and a knot tightened somewhere deep in my stomach. Kate didn’t know what really happened last summer – she especially didn’t know that I was involved – but she and I had never been close and I imagined she assumed it was all my fault anyway. Historically, if anything has gone wrong in our family Kate has always assumed I am the problem. According to her, Ismene and Amelie play so nicely when Antigone is not around, but as soon as I join in, I am like “a bull in a china shop”, “a wild child”, “a drama queen”, and turn their sweet play-times to chaos. Historically. According to Kate.

I shook off the negativity, grateful that we never had to tell Auntie Kate the full truth of Amelie’s accident.

Amelie turned the screen further towards me, saying, “Look at this stage, Tig! You can do lots of different activities, but I have done drama classes every year since I was eight. It's how I became so good at aerial silks, which is technically circus skills not drama, but at Alpine you can do pretty much *anything*! The teachers are beyond strict, but they get you doing really hard things."

It was incredible. Alpine camp took place over the school holidays and literally took over an entire boarding school! The normal teachers were switched for camp teachers, and history and maths were switched to drama and sport, but lots of the students from the school stuck around for the holidays so they could take part in camp.

I kept scrolling through the photos on the website. I couldn't believe these drama facilities belonged to a school. It was all so much more luxurious than the black box drama studio at Brinstock High. It was actually better than our professional stage. No wonder Amelie had been so unimpressed by us when she came to stay last summer! I thought of the Old Nicostrata, all sad and empty but patiently waiting for us to come home and re-open the doors to the next show.

My cheeks flushed pink. "It's huge and very—"

"Well equipped!" Issy cut straight into my sentence, zooming into the lighting rig on the screen and making mental notes of the different combinations of brilliance she would create. "The kids who go to this school are so lucky!"

I took back control of the screen and began to flick through images of past camp productions. They looked like photos from the West End or Broadway stages. (Not that I had been, but from what I had seen online!)

"It is a boarding school, so they do have to live there ten months of the year, and lots of them will even spend the school holidays at the camps too. It's not just a school; it's their home."

I flicked back to the home page and took another look at the enormous mountain ranges standing proudly to attention against a powerful blue sky. "Or prison," I muttered to myself. Could I trade freedom in Brinstock for heaven on earth but always being told what to do?

"It's not prison!" Amelie laughed and pulled back the laptop. "Most of the kids at the camp go to the school, but they are really nice. You will love them!"

"That's because *you* are really nice, Amelie. Everyone loves you." Issy's compliment landed on Amelie like fairy dust, causing her eyes to sparkle even brighter. Those two loved sharing their "cousin moments" and this one was radiating good vibes until . . .

"Yeah, sure," I muttered.

Suddenly, out of nowhere, I heard myself laughing sarcastically. Not in my head, like it was supposed to be, but actually out loud so they both heard me. They looked at me, clearly confused and a little worried by my reaction.

I tried to dig myself out of the giant hole I had just leaped into. "I mean, yeah sure you are so loveable . . . and . . . I'm not laughing in a bad way, like: ha, Amelie isn't nice. I am laughing, like: yeah, you are *so* nice. I can't believe we didn't used to be friends!" They continued to study my face. I didn't think I had convinced them, so I kept pushing through: "I'm laughing at myself. Like: Tig, how could you not know that Amelie is so nice – you're crazy!"

A pause hung awkwardly in the air. Was this the beginning of the end of our short-lived truce? Issy threw me a sister-scowl. She knew that wasn't what I was thinking. She also knew we couldn't let Amelie know that, or our fragile reconciliation would be over for good.

My sister put on her diplomatic voice decorated with the sweetest smile. "It's true, Amelie. Tig was telling me on the flight that she wishes you two had been friends since you were little, instead of having all those crazy arguments."

Good rescue, Issy!

"And she feels so *stupid* that she never gave you a chance."

I nodded emphatically and forced my eyes to look pitiful and humble. I mean, Amelie hadn't been exactly innocent in all this, but hey that was the past!

Issy kept going. "Tig told me she struggles with jealousy . . ."

Okay, Issy, that's enough! I took back control of the conversation. "I'm just so happy the three of us are friends now. Cousins and besties!" I pulled them both in for a really awkward hug and accidentally thrust my elbow into Amelie's cheek in the process. She didn't say anything, probably wanting to keep the moment sweet, but I could see her gently rubbing her face and wondering if these two weeks away together at the Alpine Adventure Youth Camp were a good idea after all.

All the energy and friendship that had been floating in the room was starting to deflate, so I scoured my brain to try and think of a change in conversation.

"You have a great bedroom, Amelie. It's really . . ." I tried to think of a fitting compliment. It shouldn't have been difficult. Her bedroom was luxuriously filled with soft toys, comfy furniture (that made me wonder why we were sitting on the floor) and glass doors leading onto her own white balcony. It was like a scene from *Romeo and Juliet*, except Juliet had a walk-in closet filled with clothes and shoes and Parisian bags.

I kept searching for that compliment. "Yeah, really . . . great!"

Amelie smiled awkwardly. I didn't need to look at Ismene. I could feel her scowl burning holes into the side of my face. I was about to blurt out some more words in the hope that they would be better than the last when my mum appeared in the doorway.

"Hello girls."

Relief! Joy! Fear! Anxiety! Nervous laughter! It all raced through my limbs at the same time like a bolt of electricity. Sometimes Mum turns up at exactly the right time and one of those times was now. She slipped easily into conversation with her niece, and I grabbed hold of the opportunity to recompose myself. I tried to take some deep breaths without anyone noticing. I shuffled around a little to make myself look carefree and nonchalant. I pulled out my phone as though I was so chilled I could just go for a scroll around the internet, because nothing weird had just happened. I looked down and saw a message from Fidge:

How's it going with Amelie? Are you still friends?

My thumb hovered across the screen as I ran a few replies through my mind: (1) I think I've offended her already; (2) this was a bad idea; (3) she hates me again.

I looked up and saw my mum enthusiastically exploring the Alpine Adventure Youth Camp website, gushing about the incredible opportunities that awaited us. "Oh look, there's an end-of-camp hike competition in the Alps. Oh girls, how thrilling! I'm sure the three of you will win. Look – you get your names engraved on a trophy. How wonderful!"

Issy and Amelie were huddled either side of her to get a closer look at the photos. I moved uncomfortably, not sure if I was still invited in on the excitement.

My mum caught a glimpse of me and sent over an affirming smile. "Tiggy, come and look at this hike competition – it's incredible." She extended her arms towards me and I felt her hug from the other side of the room.

I looked back down at my phone and went for option four:

It's all good, we're friends.

I hurried my reply and then jumped in for the family huddle on Amelie's bedroom floor.

Four

I thought I'd remembered Amelie's family dinner table as super-sized because the last time I was sitting at it I was ten and tiny. Turned out I was wrong; it was colossal! I'd been in Amelie's bedroom all afternoon and now, sitting here, waiting for Auntie Kate to come to the table, I realized how hungry I was. It wouldn't be a problem, with the amount of food laid out before us. Admittedly I'd been hoping to fill my belly with Uncle Jacques' speciality, Quiche Lorraine, which is like a creamy, cheesy, ham and bacon pie but a thousand times nicer. But my auntie and uncle had opted for a spread of Chinese takeaway and at the moment I was so hungry I could probably have eaten it all on my own.

I was stuck in a stare at the prawn crackers and debating which dish to dip them in first when Auntie Kate appeared opposite me. I instantly sat up and gave her my best smile. Her gaze landed on me briefly and she dutifully curled her lips to acknowledge that, yes, Antigone was sitting opposite her, and yes, she was smiling.

I glanced over the table towards my mum, who in turn was tentatively watching her sister.

Amelie was lucky – she got my mum as an auntie who was always giving cuddles and encouragement and oodles of attention. I had cold and frosty Kate! Sometimes, I would imagine my parents dying in a shipwreck in a wild and stormy sea heading for faraway lands and hidden treasure. I knew it wasn't the 1800s, and my parents were not treasure hunters, nor did they own a gnarly wooden pirate ship crewed by thugs and hooligans, but the point is, when they did die in my imagination, Kate always put me up for adoption! Not Ismene. No, *she* became their second daughter and the sister Amelie never had. It was just me staring at the moon through old sash windows, scrubbing floors and singing about our "hard knock life" like Annie and the other orphans. And even though sometimes, on a dark winter's morning, Aunt Kate did visit the orphanage, her intentions were wicked and she was far more Count Olaf than Mrs Weasley.

"Earth to Antigone!"

I snapped back to reality and realized my dad had been calling me from across the table.

"Could you pass me the prawn crackers, Tig?" Dad was in holiday mode already and his chilled-out smile sent a ripple of kindness my way.

I grabbed hold of the crackers and passed them to him before piling up my own plate with food. Sweet and sour chicken, steamy dumplings, chow mein, spring rolls and a mountain of fried rice. It seemed the haul of snacks I had been devouring all day had not dampened my appetite. I was so consumed by my food that I barely heard the drum of conversation steadily beating in the background. I did, however, hear my name being mentioned.

"So you're still using a knife and fork, Tig?" It was Auntie Kate, who was staring at me through familiar piercing blue eyes – the same sparkly blue Issy and Amelie had stolen from the gene pool. Her hair fell over her shoulders in soft blonde locks and rested gently on a white silk shirt.

"Huh?" I asked, stroking my hair flat and trying to remember if I'd brushed it that morning.

"I notice you still haven't learned to use chopsticks?"

I looked around the dinner table and realized I was the only one using metal cutlery. I squirmed a little in my seat and feigned a short laugh. I hoped she was trying to be funny. Kate's eyes refused to move away from me. I held my breath as she looked me up and down, clearly conducting some kind of analysis on me. I looked around the table to try and find a friendly face. Everyone was occupied with their feast, dipping delicate wooden chopsticks into their dishes and delivering the food precisely to their mouths.

Everyone except my mum. While I sat under the hostile gaze of Auntie Kate, my mum was watching her sister like a crocodile handler, ready to bring her older sibling under control the moment she snapped. My eyes darted between them both. I tried to figure out whether the chopsticks question was rhetorical or if my aunt was actually expecting an answer, but Kate pushed further.

"You are going to need to work a little harder on your table manners if you want to fit in at Alpine."

"Kate." My mum muttered a warning under her breath, but Kate was unfazed.

"I am helping her out, Laura. Swiss customs around cuisine are even more defined than the French."

I smiled at my auntie and tried to end the conversation. "That's okay, I pick things up quickly."

Kate took a breath, ready to deliver her comeback, but my dad's booming voice pulled everyone's attention his way. "You sure do!" he said to me, before adding: "I honestly can't thank you both enough for paying for the girls to go along with Amelie. It's all they've talked about."

Uncle Jacques waved his hand dismissively to make sure we all knew it was no big deal.

Kate said, "Amelie has been begging to spend time with her cousins and this seems the only way to ensure they are together in a safe environment." Kate leaned in on the word "safe" and my mum shifted awkwardly on her seat.

Amelie and Issy sat closely together at the opposite end of the table to me. (I made a note to self: always wait for them to sit down first so I can go and join them!) Talk of Alpine pulled Amelie into the conversation. "You are going to love it so much. Tig, you should learn silks. I can teach you some things if you like?"

I went to answer, but Issy got in first. "I want to learn silks!"

They both giggled and chattered into each other and I deeply regretted not being at their end of the table. I made sure I spoke extra loudly to keep hold of my cousin's attention. "I can't wait to try it. I've been watching tutorials online – it looks hard!"

Auntie Kate let out one of those laughs that grown-ups do when they want you to know they think you are ridiculous. "Well yes, anything that's worth anything is hard work, Antigone. Amelie has been training in aerial silks for years."

I looked over at my mum, who soothed me with a knowing smile. Dad, still musing on his gratitude towards my aunt and uncle, said: "You might discover it's your new passion. Imagine aerial silks as a permanent fixture at the Old Nic!"

There was an abrupt silence. Did my dad really just say that? Had he completely forgotten about last summer and Amelie's Ariel Silk performance that very nearly killed my cousin, leaving a distraught family, sealing the fate of our family theatre as being for ever shut and landing me with a life sentence in prison?

My mum eyeballed my dad, subtly asking him to rein in his excitement. "Let's not get ahead of ourselves. This week is about trying new things and having fun." Her eyes darted between Dad and Kate, hoping her words were enough to close down the one conversation everyone was trying so hard to avoid.

"I wouldn't do that. Look what happened last time." Except Kate, of course. *She* was really happy to go there. In fact, she looked pleased. I was pretty sure she had been hoping for this conversation ever since we arrived. She kept pushing: "Aerial silks requires safety and precision, and clearly that is not Antigone's forte. Perhaps the Old Nic should stick to pranks and pantos for now."

Wow, Auntie Kate really knows how to throw shade. So this was where Amelie got her quick-thinking, mean-girl remarks from. Her mother was a pro!

I sat up in my seat and took a determined breath. *I must not rise to the negativity* . . . I could shake it off.

I was getting good at shaking off bad vibes. I looked again towards my mum. Her head hung a little lower and her lips tightened. I could hear Kate ranting in the background, mixed with the low hum of Amelie and Issy laughing, both unaware of the rising tension at the table. I turned my attention to my parents, each staring quietly into empty dinner plates. They looked like a pair of naughty children being reprimanded for misbehaving at the dinner table.

A wild rush of indignation swirled through my body. *Do not say a word; just smile and let it all blow over.* I swallowed back the urge to defend my parents from the subtle insults coming their way, but Kate was still talking and every sentence was weighing them down. I pulled my eyes away, not wanting to watch them be crushed by my aunt. And I focused on Kate. I listened. I heard the cruel words she was saying out loud *and* the unspoken ones, hidden in her silences.

"Running a business is a huge responsibility. Perhaps it should have stayed shut!"

My hands were feeling sweaty. I tried to swallow, but there was a heavy pulsating in my throat.

Kate was furiously piling her plate with more rice, still ranting at my parents. "You play around as though life is a game and when things get serious it is always left for one of us to come and rescue you."

My parents were not saying anything. They were not eating anything. It didn't even look as if they were breathing. My chest was beating harder and harder, and under the table my feet were bouncing up and down. My whole body was ready to pounce.

"I know we said we wouldn't talk about it, but the truth is you did very nearly kill our daughter."

The word "kill" stabbed through my chest like an arrow. But no one was looking at me. Issy and Amelie were still deep in chatter, unaware of the battleground being marked across the table. Jacques was thrusting food into his mouth and nodding in agreement with every word Kate said. My dad was starting to fidget awkwardly, but my mum was frozen still. I looked back to Kate, her red lips and white teeth had become a deadly weapon, throwing missiles across the table.

"You act like some wonderful mother who always has time for the little children. But you are negligent, foolish, incapable of . . ."

I couldn't listen to another word. Someone had to make her stop! My head understood the importance of me being quiet and leaving the grown-ups to sort things out. Unfortunately, my mouth and heart don't often listen to my brain at times like this. My voice shaking and cheeks flushed red, I thrust myself to my feet and screamed out above the noise, "Leave her alone! It wasn't Mum's fault. It was me. I nearly killed Amelie!"

A ripple of breathless gasps was followed by silence.

Five

I had been asked to leave the table. Actually, I'd been savagely kicked out in a double attack led by both Uncle Jacques and Auntie Kate. I tried to smooth things over and explain how Amelie's accident happened, but all they seemed to hear was, *I tried to murder your daughter and I will definitely do it again!*

They were still shouting now, only this time my parents were not trying to keep the peace. From the small spare room, which was now my room because the sleepover had been cancelled, for me at least, I could hear the raised voices and odd phrases making their way through the gap under the door.

"You should have told us the truth," Kate said.

Mum replied: "*Listen!* You are making this sound like something it's not."

"I know exactly what this is. It's *that girl* causing problems AGAIN."

Dad admitted, "We know she isn't always the easiest—"

"No!" interrupted Mum. "We are not letting Tig absorb all the blame. This was an equal argument that escalated between the girls."

"Yes, really equal," said Kate. "But it was only *my* daughter that ended up fighting for her life in hospital!"

Jacques jumped in. "Kate and I have seen the film footage, Laura. You and Kevin need to know—"

"It was an ACCIDENT," shouted Mum. "She didn't mean to do it; she was overwhelmed—"

"Oh, she was overwhelmed . . . SHE IS ALWAYS OVERWHELMED!"

My Dad, always the voice of reason, spoke again, "Antigone is a good girl with a good heart. She never meant to hurt Amelie."

"But she *did* hurt Amelie. Just like she always *does* one way or another, with her incessant wild behaviour. Are we supposed to sit quietly and allow this girl to—"

"It was an accident," Mum repeated. "They had *both* been arguing. Kate, you know—"

"Yes, I know all right! We are all supposed to overlook Antigone's 'issues'."

There was a pause. I was waiting for my parents to throw another come-back and defend me, but the next person to speak was my aunt. "That girl is reckless, impulsive and completely unsafe. She is a menace to this family."

Dad replied: "Now, Kate—"

"Well, she is!"

There was a deathly quiet and no matter how close I pushed my ear to the gap under the door, I couldn't hear a thing. I lay on the soft green carpet and allowed the draught to slowly freeze my fingers and toes. *They are horrible. I have the worst family.*

I pictured Amelie and Issy snuggled up and enjoying our sleepover without me. A pain darted into my throat and I tried to put the image out of my mind. I struggled to remember what they were doing during the argument. Had they still been laughing and chatting, or did they look as horrified as the adults? One thing I did know was that Amelie never defended me. She didn't try to contextualize the row or confess to her part in it all.

I rolled up off the carpet and collapsed into the bed. I imagined Amelie and Issy again, but this time they were gossiping – about me.

I hate it here. I hate the stupid camp. I hate my stupid family. Wet tears started to trickle down my cheeks and into my hair. Why was everyone always so mad at me? Why did I always end up in trouble? A loud sob leapt out of my throat, followed by another and another. I cried until my head hurt.

I pulled my knees up to my chest. The curtains were open, and outside the street was empty. A cat walked confidently across the road before slipping under a warm parked car. I thought of Taco sitting outside our empty house and hoped Fidge had remembered to give him night-time snuggles. I missed Taco, I missed Fidge, I wanted to go home.

As sleep crept up on me a persistent thought fluttered around my mind. Kate did not want me to be near Amelie, and Mum didn't want to be near Kate. We would be going home in the morning. Camp would probably have been rubbish anyway. Just another few weeks of being told what to do . . . and getting into trouble for doing it wrong . . . and upsetting all the kids without knowing why. Relief softened my body as I sank deeper into my pillow. It had been a great idea, but it was never going to happen. Camp would be cancelled. I'd be back home by the end of tomorrow.

Six

Sure, I would miss Amelie, but I'd been on the planet for thirteen years. Thirteen whole years of being cousins with Amelie and in all that time we had only been friends for eight months! Our history as enemies far exceeded any friendship.

I spat toothpaste into the sink and swirled cold water around my mouth. This morning was going to be tough. Ismene would be devastated not to go to camp. She and Amelie had been friends their whole lives. A pang of guilt pulled at my chest and I quickly washed it away by throwing cold water into my face. I looked back up into the mirror. Rings encircled my eyes, and my cheeks were still puffy from the night before. I grabbed a hair band and pulled my hair into a short, scrappy ponytail.

A few years from now, when we were all adults and our parents were old and busy doing old people stuff, the three of us would be friends again. Me, Amelie and Issy. We would travel Europe together. Or America! We would start at the Grand Canyon and end in New York.

I paused and studied my reflection to see if I really believed me.

Six

I'm going home today. I can figure everything else out another time.

Packing was as easy as returning my toothbrush to my bag. Admittedly, I was wearing the same clothes I'd travelled in *and* slept in, which was pretty gross. I looked down and saw a tiny stain from last night's Chinese takeaway and considered at least switching it for another sweater. I sniffed the pink wool and detected a faint whisper of the night before. It was a sharp enough reminder that the main priority right now was getting home. I could change into something fresh when I was in *my* room with *my* cat and no one was judging me.

I shuffled down the stairs and left my case by the front door. Issy's suitcase was packed and ready to go, which meant she was even more eager to leave than I was! A little lump swelled up in my throat as tears of gratitude stung the backs of my eyes. She was a good sister. Issy was so close to Amelie, but when the battle lines were drawn, it was always going to be me and her, sisters first! I drew in a long breath, filling my lungs with confidence and determination, then made my way into the kitchen.

"Antigone, sweetheart, come here for a cuddle. I am so sorry my evil sister spoke so cruelly to you last night. She is wicked and we will never let her near you again.

Come on, darling, let's go home." That was what I was expecting Mum to say! And then Dad would come to me with a bandage on his hand, looking a little bit guilty, before saying, "And Jacques won't be bothering you again either." And then I would look at Amelie weeping in the corner, so embarrassed by her family but at least knowing that in five years' time Ismene and I would rescue her and we would travel the world together.

But what the . . .

My mum was making pancakes *with* Kate! Amelie had a yellow T-shirt on with the words "Alpine Adventure Youth Camp" emblazoned across it – clearly she was still going! My eyes darted around the room trying to piece the puzzle together. Issy! My sister, yes *sister*, was teaching Uncle Jacques how to do something on his laptop, and Dad, well, actually he was just drinking coffee, but still – drinking coffee on a day like today? Felt kind of treacherous to me.

Nobody seemed to have noticed my arrival and I considered slipping back out of the room. But no! I was tired of always being the one to leave. I rooted my bare feet a little more firmly to the cold kitchen tiles before projecting my voice above the kitchen chatter. "I am ready to go now!" Everyone's eyes turned on me and I saw a sea of smiling faces. No one said anything, so I tried again. "I am ready to go now!"

My mum smiled as she offered me a plate of pancakes and a warm mug of tea. The pancakes already had syrup and fresh strawberries on them and a surge of happiness whizzed around my heart as I took in the smell. She knew this would happen. Mum was playing me.

Stand firm, Antigone.

"No thanks. I'll eat when I get home."

My mum went to say something and then paused. The kitchen fell quiet until my dad let out a little chuckle. "There'll be nothing left of you after three weeks!"

My heart started to pick up its pace as the sweet joy of pancakes began to evaporate. I knew Mum could feel the anxiety prickling under my skin. I knew she would do anything she could to halt it. Her face turned serious, and she pulled her shoulders back. "Antigone, your auntie Kate has something to say to you."

Kate had an apron on. She had her hair swept up into a relaxed messy bun and was wearing a dusky pink tracksuit obviously made from a lustrous blend of silk and cashmere and completely inappropriate for doing sport in. She was *smiling* at me.

She walked around the posh island in the middle of the kitchen and stood close to me before resting her hand gently on my shoulder, saying, "I'm sorry, Tig. I was rude to you last night. Your mum explained what happened between you and Amelie. She also told me about how you tried to put things right by visiting the police and writing down your thoughts and feelings. I hear you are managing to make some very positive changes in your behaviour too."

Her face was so pretty and her touch so gentle that I really wanted to believe her. My lip quivered a little, but I couldn't decide whether to feel angry, relieved or completely betrayed.

There was a light touch on my other shoulder as my mum joined us. "I know last night was a tough start to the trip and you probably want to turn around and go straight back home, right?"

I locked my jaw tightly and nodded just enough to confirm my wishes without allowing any of my suppressed tears to bubble through my hard stare.

"I don't want you to miss out on camp, and neither does Amelie or Issy."

"Nor do I! Jolly good opportunity!" my dad called over his coffee. He was doing that thing where he lightens the mood by pretending to be oblivious to all the tension in the room.

I tightened my jaw further, still not sure which emotion would lead my response.

My mum captured the shift in atmosphere. "Great! So that's settled then. Let's get these pancakes eaten up and then we can make our way to the airport."

Issy let out a squeal of excitement. "Eeeeek! Switzerland, here we come!"

I didn't know what to say. Or what to think. Or what to do. A plate of pancakes was placed in my hands and everyone was back doing whatever was occupying them when I first came in.

Okay, so I'm going to Switzerland. And apparently last night never even happened . . .

Mum looked at me through a swirling cloud of steam rising from the kettle. She smiled and gave me a wink. I guess that meant, *Great, all sorted, let's forget it ever happened.* But I was not sure it was all sorted. I didn't think I was ready to forget either. I tried hard to enjoy the pancakes, but they seemed to have turned to stone, and swallowing felt like a curse.

I hope you know what you're doing, Mum, because I think you have made a horrible mistake.

Seven

I had five minutes before we left for the airport. I ripped off my day-old clothes and pulled out something clean and comfy to put on. My hair was just about managing to stay up in a scrappy mess, so it would have to do – there was no time to waste on looking pretty. I had two weeks at camp and another in Paris with my family. That was three whole weeks of holding things together. Things *could* go well, but that wasn't what my gut was telling me.

I scrambled my hands blindly through my travel bag, searching for the only reliable friend I had with me right now. The one thing I knew I could be honest with.

I pulled out the notebook and hurried past the first few pages. I had been so positive just a week ago. I landed on a blank page. I had hoped I would never need to write about my tangled-up life again, but deep down I always knew I would.

I pulled out a pen and started to scribble.

Hey notebook,

It's me again – Tig. Nothing has really happened yet . . . apart from being in a foreign country and on my way to another completely foreign country, having spent the evening in a major battle with my family that apparently never happened and having to eat pancakes that felt like eating rocks. But, apart from that, I have this feeling that something very, very bad is about to happen. I don't understand what's going on or why everyone is acting the way they are. I don't know how I am supposed to feel or behave . . .

"Tig! We're leaving!" My sister was yelling to me from downstairs. Everyone was probably in the car already.

"Just a minute!" I yelled back.

Don't judge me, okay. I am doing my best. I will do my best. I will go to camp with a can-do attitude and become Amelie's greatest protégé on aerial silks. I will be friendly and positive and hard working . . .

"Tiggy, I am getting in the car NOW." Dad was trying to give me a friendly nudge, but I could hear his frustration.

"On my way!" I just needed a few more minutes.

I will be exactly the way they all want me to be. I just need to figure out what that is . . .

"Antigone!" My mum's head appeared from behind the door. She looked just as frustrated, flustered and confused as me. "What are you doing? Everyone is waiting for you. Come on!"

She didn't wait for an answer. I knew I was out of time.

Three weeks and I will be back home. Three weeks, that's all. So why do I feel like something terrible is about to happen?

PART TWO

Eight ♡

"I'm sorry, sweetie, but your name isn't on this list either."

I ran my eyes down the page for the fifteenth time. I couldn't find Antigone, Tig, Tiggy, not even "other Kingsley girl from England" – *nothing*!

"Okay, we need to speak with Admin, see what's going on."

Jada's black, spiralled hair shimmied down her back as she found a clearing in the crowds to make *another* phone call. I had been at Alpine Adventure Youth Camp for two hours and this kind, twenty-something youth worker from Seattle had quickly become my only ally. I watched as she paced up and down in the corner of the main hall, her hand blocking one ear as she tried to understand the person on the other end of the phone.

There were teenagers everywhere. In my school, we all look the same, sound the same, wear the same uniform. But the meeting hall at Alpine Adventure Youth Camp was a sea of unfamiliar sounds and faces. We all looked a similar age, as in we had managed to grow to similar heights and statures, but these guys had a sense of certainty and worldly wisdom that seemed to have forgotten me and my mates in Brinstock. I pulled my shoulders back and pretended to smile. Trying to look confident and chilled out in a place like that was tough, especially when it was two hours into camp and still nobody seemed to have any record of me.

"Tig!"

I followed the sound of my name and saw Amelie and Issy weaving their way through the crowds, their eyes alive with excitement and hands filled with stuff.

"Tig, look, our dorm room has a gift-bag on every bed. I have chocolate, a notebook, a team tee with my name on the back . . ."

Issy was glowing, linking her arm into Amelie's, who looked like the one who makes everyone's dreams come true. I looked down at their bright yellow tops with the word "DRAMA" emblazoned on the front. A knot formed in my throat and the fact I was dorm-less and gift-bag-less and yellow-tee-labelled-"DRAMA"-less suddenly became a really big problem to me.

"Is there a bed with my name on it in the room?" My voice sounded harsher than I had intended, but *that* was what they had promised to check. In the two seconds it took for them both to get signed in on the register and receive directions to their dorm, they promised me the first thing they would do was check for a bed labelled "Antigone". I looked at their blank, perhaps a little guilty, faces and felt a flash of annoyance mixed with dread.

Issy must have noticed, as she quickly stepped into her big sister role. "Don't panic, it's not like you will be thrown out of camp. They have your name somewhere and I am sure they will just bunk you in with us."

I wanted to agree with her but the long history of things not working out for me whenever Issy and Amelie were together made it hard to believe.

"*Amélie, comment ça va?*"

A movement in the crowd toppled me into another group of strangers as three more yellow tee-shirts joined Amelie and Issy. Amelie squealed in excitement as hugs and high-fives rippled around their little huddle. The moment I heard French I knew it was time to find Jada. I reorientated myself back to where she had left me and saw her still on the phone. I wove my way through the crowds to join her. I felt flat and fed up. It was four in the afternoon and in the last twenty-four hours I had experienced the full spectrum of human emotion. If Jada had handed me a ticket straight back home – not back to my parents in Paris, but to my *home*, where Taco and Fidge were hanging out and eating lasagna or whatever – I would have been totally okay with it.

"Okay, Tig, mystery solved!" Jada placed an affirming hand on my shoulder, and I fought the urge to go in for a cuddle. She flicked to another page in her folder. "We have been looking at the wrong faculty. Look, your name isn't enrolled for drama. You are here in pottery class."

There was a long pause. Jada waited for me to smile with relief. I waited for her to explain why on earth my name would be on a page for kids learning pottery. Noticing my lack of enthusiasm, she tentatively continued, "So you are with the brown shirts, and your dorm is over there to the left. Shall I come with you?"

I stared at her for a moment, hoping she would come up with another solution, but she offered nothing, so I said, "Look, Jada, I don't do pottery; there must be a mistake. I don't actually like . . . I mean, it's not my *thing*, you know?"

Jada nodded compassionately, but I could see she was withholding something. Then she said, "You know, pottery camp is a lot of fun and you get to make some awesome dishes and things out of clay. And I know some of the kids on that course. They are great – you're gonna have a blast."

I pulled myself up and tried to assert some authority. "I appreciate your help, but no! I am a drama kinda girl and definitely not a clay kinda girl. So you can take my name off the brown shirts and move it to the yellow. Please."

Jada looked anxiously around the room before guiding me even further into the corner and away from the crowds. She lowered her voice so no prying ears could hear our conversation. "Antigone, the office spoke to Kate Toussant last night. That's your mum, right?"

My whole body turned to stone as the memory of my aunt made the whole situation one hundred times worse. "No, she is my auntie."

"Right, well, she is in charge of your booking, and she has requested that you be taken off drama and placed into pottery instead."

Wow, Auntie Kate must hate me so much. "But why? I came for drama. I have to do drama. I don't want to make pottery!"

Jada's shoulders rounded slightly and I could feel her face mirror my own. "I don't know, sweetie. There were some concerns that you may become overwhelmed and this would be the best option for everyone."

A familiar bubble of anger began boiling up inside me, with a long list of things to be raging about.

1. Kate sent me here knowing I would have a horrible time.
2. Jada, who seemed really nice, now thought I had anger issues or suffered from overwhelm or whatever.
3. I had to spend two weeks making stinking pottery.
4. Did my parents know?

I swallowed down my fury and clenched my jaw tight in the hope that neither anger nor tears would escape.

Jada gently put her arm around my shoulder. "Let me take you to your dorm. The girls there are super-nice, and pottery might be more fun than you think."

I felt completely lost. I didn't trust myself to speak and I could see I had no other options. Jada was the only friend I had, and following her was the only thing I could do.

Nine

As the door to the dorm room closed behind Jada, I felt like a little kid being abandoned on the first day of school. I'd been hoping to arrive at an empty room with plenty of time and space to process the last forty-eight hours. Instead, I was confronted with three eager sets of eyes staring into mine, just ten inches from my face.

"We have been stood here for three hours waiting for you." A girl with deep brown eyes and silky brown hair trailing down her sides stared at me with readable expectation. In her hands was an iPad, and facing towards me on the screen was a blonde girl staring with equal anticipation. The third girl looked out behind a mass of wavy orange hair and bright orange freckles. She was smiling, giving me hope that she felt her three-hour wait was worth it.

My eyes scoured the room quickly, hoping to find a space to call my own and retreat to, but the eyes were still upon me and waiting for an answer.

"Okay." It was the best I could do.

The brown-haired girl was simmering with energy. She took a step even closer, narrowing the distance between us even more. "I am Talia. *Soy española. ¿Has estado en España? ¿Hablas español? ¿Te gusta España?*"

I had no idea what she was saying but her voice was a little louder and a little higher with every word. I looked towards Freckles to see if she could translate or elaborate, but she just stared at me through big, round, hazelnut eyes.

Talia jumped in again: "It's okay, we don't need to speak Spanish. We can speak English if you prefer, or French, of course, or German. Teresa is German, so sometimes we speak that too."

I looked down at the screen in Talia's hands and watched as the blonde girl, Teresa I guessed, nodded emphatically.

Talia kept talking: "This is Teresa. She was supposed to come, because she comes every year, but last night she got the tonsillitis, and her parents say she must not come." Talia spoke with a soft Spanish accent that made every word sound really cute.

There was another long pause and the eyes in front of me all seemed hopeful I was going to fill it. "Okay . . ." Admittedly I wasn't doing so well.

Talia edged a little closer once more. "Okay and this is Tony."

My gaze landed on the freckle-faced, orange-haired girl in front of me. She was silent but, just like Talia, looked as though she was about to burst out of her skin. I tried to ease her anticipation a little: "Hi Tony, nice to meet you."

Talia jumped in. "Tony no, *Tony*."

"Toh-nee," I replied, because honestly, it all sounded exactly the same.

A little giggle escaped from Freckles, and Talia ramped up her explanation. "Too–nee, not Tony like Antonio, but Tony like the howl."

She was trying so hard but all I could hear was, "Not TONY, but Tony like the howl!?" I searched my brain trying to make sense of what she was saying. How was it we were speaking English and I was the one who was confused? I looked to Teresa on the screen, who was silently laughing, and then back to Freckles, desperately hoping someone else would offer an answer.

Talia continued, "You know – Tooonnnyyy . . . like Tony howl? This is her – she has this name."

Just then Tony Howl decided it was time to speak. "I'm Tawny, like the owl. A tawny owl."

Utter relief shimmied down my body as I heard a faint American accent rustle through the quiet tones of Tawny's voice.

"Yes, like I said: Tony Howl."

Talia was still talking but my focus had fixed on Tawny. She was the English speaker here. I would be needing her. "So, Tawny, are you American?" I tried to sound casual, like her speaking English was no big deal, but I had a little happy dance going on inside.

"No, I am Danish, but I always go to international schools, so I kinda sound American."

If there had been any space between me and the three sets of eyes, I would have shrunk back a little the moment I discovered I was the only one who didn't speak at least three languages. But there was no space and the eyes were still looking at me like something crazy was about to happen. What were they expecting? Did they want me to sing? Should I have prepared a speech?

Noticing my awkward silence, Talia dived back in as the group leader. "Okay, so to explain, she is Teresa, she is Tony and I am Talia. You see?" Her eyes were alive with excitement as they all waited for me to understand whatever joke they were peddling.

I tried to figure out what the big deal was, but it wasn't really happening. "Yes, nice to meet you."

Talia kept pushing. "Teresa, Tony, Talia . . . the three Ts! This is what they call us!"

All three girls let out a suppressed giggle and I began to realize that this was the big reveal they had been desperate to make. I tried to join them with a little fake laugh and I thought for a moment I had pulled it off, but after a few more seconds of pretend laughing, awkwardness still hung in the air like a bad smell and I could see they wanted more.

"Oh, okay! That's great, yeah, three Ts. So funny." I tried, I really did. I even gave a thumbs-up to show them how much I approved of their group name.

There was another pause. I was hoping, now that the joke was finished, they would move out of the way and let me into my new room, but Tawny stared at me intensely, like this was the moment she had been waiting for. She took a deep breath before asking me in a squeakily quiet voice, "So, we've been wondering, and *hoping*, that maybe you'll be a T too."

I glanced across to Teresa, who was still avidly waiting for my reply. Talia jumped back in with, "So, what *is* your name?"

All three put their hands together, as though they were ardently praying and hoping for something really significant. Something way more important than the first letter of my name. Feeling completely confused and a tiny bit amused by my new camp mates I decided to put them out of their misery. "I am Antigone."

It was as though there was an actual bubble that I had actually burst. All of the deep expectation in the room seeped out like air from a deflated balloon. Talia dramatically threw her arms up and Tawny slumped her shoulders in disappointment. I couldn't see Teresa as the iPad was being swirled around in Talia's utter sadness at hearing my name. The three Ts had gone from level ten (total elation) to minus one (devastatingly miserable).

I tried to offer some comfort. "Well, you know, pretty much everyone calls me Tig, so . . ."

There was a moment of silence once again, as Talia, Tawny and Teresa all paused to register my shortened name. And, once again, I had never seen a room change its energy so quickly. They didn't just return to level-ten elation. These guys were off-the-scale jubilation. There was jumping, squealing, dancing, even chanting: "The Ts, the Ts, the Ts."

I laughed in my head, a lot, but on the outside I used the hysteria to move from the doorway to what looked like the one remaining unclaimed bed. I sat down tentatively and put my bag on my lap. Celebrations seemed to be going on a really long time. Weirdly long. I had never shared a dorm room with strangers before. I had never been away from home before. I couldn't even recall a time I had been in the same room as people from multiple countries. What surprised me more than any of this was that I had been housed with three girls who were even more crazy than me.

I would love to tell you how the rest of the evening

was all "get to know each other" chats, face packs and clothes-swapping, but the reality was quite different. The three Ts had their long-established friendship rituals to execute, which included a card game, slideshow presentations of their past year, and posh food that in my world only the grown-ups would eat. For a solid group of besties, they were kind and invited me to join them in every activity – I was the new "T", after all! But I felt ridiculous. I was stuck in a room with three girls I barely knew (yes, Teresa stayed with us online all night) and who seemed to get excited by the most boring things. I didn't want to be their fourth T, I didn't want to eat their strange food and I really really didn't want to make stinking pottery.

With two weeks of camp ahead of me I crawled under my luxurious covers and held my breath as a few silent tears rolled down my cheeks. I wanted to run and see Amelie and Issy, but I was angry with them for not coming to see me first. I wanted to call my parents, but I was *furious* at them for letting Auntie Kate send me to pottery classes. For a few moments my thumbs poised over Fidge's phone number, ready to send an angry download about why my family were rubbish and I hated the letter T. But as the night drew on and Tawny's snoring became louder, I convinced myself that I was alone. Utterly and miserably alone.

Ten

My feet fizzed with numbness. I tried to wriggle them around, but there was a heavy load holding my toes hostage under the bed covers. Taco! I assumed it had been cold the night before and my fur-ball cat must have crept into my room for a snuggle. Knowing that cats love to be comfy but hate to be disturbed, I nudged my legs slightly, expecting him to spring to his feet. He didn't budge. Nothing really moved, because it wasn't Taco. My dreamy brain flicked through all of the possible options, calmly trying to decide who was perched at the end of my bed. Maybe Ismene, and I was late for school again. Maybe my parents, and they were apologizing for sending me to camp.

The mere thought of the word "camp" conjured up a weighty reality in my mind: *Ugh, that's right. I am at camp.*

I was about to head down a long trail of sadness, reliving all the injustice I had experienced in my first day at camp, when the thought hit me again: *I am at CAMP! So what* is *on the end of my bed?*

My eyes opened just enough to see a small figure surrounded by an orange halo glaring down at me. I let out a weird low yelp and shuffled up in bed as fast as I could.

"Careful, Tiggy Tig Tig. I don't want to spill your tea."

I looked in absolute horror at Tawny perched on the end of my bed, dressed in her brown camp T-shirt and staring intently at me. If this *had* been my sister, or anyone I had known for at least two days, I might have laughed. But it was *Tawny*, the girl I had spoken ten sentences to at most. I had a lot of questions for this wide-eyed human, but it was too early and too soon for my mouth to formulate words. We stared at each other for a few disconcerting seconds.

"Good morning." Her voice was strong and ready for the day as a little smile edged into the corners of her lips.

"Hi," I croaked back, hoping that was enough conversation and she would now leave.

"You need to start your day, sleepy head, so I brought you tea. Brits like tea, right?"

I awkwardly shuffled up in bed, my feet still fizzing with numbness. "Yeah, thanks."

Tawny handed me a purple mug and, grateful for the distraction, I took a giant gulp. I shuddered in disgust. It was cold. Gloopy and cold. Tawny looked at me knowingly. "I have been waiting a really long time. You must have been so tired."

I had no response. This was too strange, even for me. A stranger had made me tea and then sat on the end of my bed, watching and waiting for me to wake up and drink the tea. I was drinking cold, gloopy tea with a stranger . . . sitting on my *bed*!

I put the tea on the little cabinet next to the bed and swung my feet to the floor. "Okay. Thanks. I am going to get ready."

I left the strange, orange-haloed girl where she was and escaped into the bathroom. Catching a glimpse at myself in the mirror I took a long deep breath, muttering, "Two weeks; it's just two weeks."

Ten minutes later I left the dorm with a T on each arm. Tawny was light and I could barely feel her touch as her tiny arm rested in mine. On the other side was Talia, talking endlessly. "Always in camp there are really very many people who know each other, so you are lucky to already find us. We won't let you be alone. You are a T now. Tony and I will look out for you."

Her voice followed me all the way to the art studio. "Tiggy Tig Tig, you can sit here in the middle, can't she, Tony? And also very many people have their own pottery tools, so you can just use mine and Tony's."

She didn't slow down for a response. I looked at Tawny. Her wide eyes glared openly back at me, but she didn't seem to have anything to say. More and more people trailed into the art studio and found themselves a seat on a hard wooden stool. Talia talked incessantly. ". . . and this one year, at camp, I made seventeen mugs and seventeen plates, and on the last day I dropped one and I was so sad because. . ."

My body stayed wedged between the Ts, but my brain took a long walk around the art studio. The room was warm and bright, with high ceilings and polished wooden floors. Shelves ran across the walls, filled with sculptures, pots and ornaments. They looked good, but of course I wouldn't know, because I had never cared less about pottery! I let out a little moan and went on a friend hunt instead – someone to endure these long and boring two weeks with.

There were fifteen other students, or campers, or inmates – whatever you want to call them. Each sat in isolation. Each with music in their ears or staring like a lost soul sucked into a phone vortex. I scanned each one of them for possible friend capabilities, but the room was a crowd of loners, except the Ts. They were . . . they were from another planet! I squirmed a little on my chair, feeling completely out of place and horribly aware of Tawny still staring at me, that little smile still wedged on her face.

A flurry of energy burst into the art studio as a young woman in dungarees and a bandana breezed to the front of the class. There was a disinterested silence from most of the students but, of course, Talia had something to say. "This is Miss Tanner." She paused and smiled at me knowingly. "So, you see why we love her, right?" Talia's eyes were dancing with excitement as I tried to figure out what she wanted me to say.

"She looks really nice. I like her . . . scarf."

"Tanner! Miss *Tanner*! She is a T, Tiggy Tig Tig, like us!"

I tried to muster some enthusiasm and pretend I found the first letter of Miss Tanner's name completely hilarious too. It was exhausting.

"She is from Santa Fe, which is amazing. I was there for a summer a few years back and the art there was so inspired. I felt Miss Tanner's influence, actually. It was incredible . . ."

I looked across to my new mentor and guide on this bizarre pottery journey I had been thrown into. Her hair was hidden under a tie-dyed bandana, with little wisps of purple and pink escaping between the edges. I could imagine her ruling the streets of Santa Fe with a pottery wheel. I say *imagine*, because unlike Talia and the rest of the kids at Alpine Adventure Youth Camp, my summers were spent at home in Brinstock, with my cat, best buddy and a theatre filled with costumes, props and crazy ideas. Just another difference between me and the kids at Alpine to make me feel completely out of place!

I took a deep breath and refocused my mind. Okay, Miss Tanner looked cool, down to earth, maybe a little fun. The rest of the kids might be odd, but that was fine. I could just hang out with Miss Tanner!

Miss Tanner stepped confidently into the middle of the art studio. Her eyes scanned the array of students before her, seemingly pleased with her new cohorts. She couldn't have been much older than thirty, definitely young enough for a chilled-out chat once the rest of the guys got to work. I could let her see some of my prank videos. She would probably follow JustTigging. Perhaps then she could tell me a bit about pottery, in a less intense way than Talia. I might even learn something!

Miss Tanner took a deep breath and I confidently waited to hear her casually welcome us to class. "Today you are no longer just *you*. You are apprentices about to embark on a journey that will connect you with the very essence of creation . . ." Okay, maybe not.

"You will discover how humble lumps of clay have the potential to become not just vessels of beauty but vessels of the soul."

The room was silent. I glanced towards Talia, who had finally stopped talking. She was captivated, listening to Miss Tanner as if this teacher from Santa Fe was about to reveal the meaning of life.

"Consider form and symmetry as your guiding stars on this artistic voyage. Seek harmony through the delicate dance of shape and proportion . . ."

I lost it then. I had never heard anyone speak so passionately about a lump of clay. I let out a little giggle, trying to figure out if cool Miss Tanner was winding us up, but the whole class remained focused on her every word. I looked over to Tawny, who was wide-eyed and ready, poised to pounce on her ball of clay and work it into something other-worldly.

Miss Tanner kept speaking, each word more cryptic and confusing than the last. "Embrace these principles, and you'll unlock the secrets to crafting pieces that resonate with both the eye and the heart . . ."

I breathed awkwardly. Before I arrived at Alpine I'd had no interest in playing with dough and I felt completely okay with that. But listening to Miss Tanner talk about eyes and hearts and symmetry made me feel like an art fraud. I dipped lower in my chair hoping to stay unnoticed.

"I promise you, by the end of this class, you will discover the magic that lies within this earthy medium known in its simplest form as clay."

Silence. You could have heard a mouse fart! She walked across to her desk and picked up a large lump of clay. She stared at it for a moment before thrusting it in the air like Rafiki presenting baby Simba to the African plains at the start of *The Lion King*. Immediately, my brain burst into silent singing as the opening line from "Circle of Life" played full volume in my head: *Cats in pyjamas eating bananas...* (By the way, I know those aren't the actual lyrics, but when I was five it made so much more sense to me that it kind of stuck!)

While the almost-lyrics were looping around my brain, everyone else picked up their balls of clay and mirrored Miss Tanner's dramatic move. I watched like a spectator, a little amused, feeling very awkward, but mostly still silently singing "Circle of Life". There was another long pause – maybe it was seconds, perhaps minutes, but when I finally came out of singing in my head, everyone was staring at me. Miss Tanner's eyes glared through a small set of glasses, analyzing my face with curiosity and indignation. She wanted something from me. I wasn't sure what, but I knew it probably wasn't to know more about my YouTube channel.

"You have to take the clay! Like this!"

I looked at Talia, who was helpfully nodding towards a ball of clay in front of me, her arms thrust out and hands filled with her own "magical" clay. I grabbed hold of the ball and lifted it in the air. It wasn't funny, but I couldn't hold back little giggles bubbling out of my mouth. I took a deep breath and tried to look really serious, but the song started playing in my head again, and I was doing some weird sort of clay worship, and if Fidge was here he would find the whole thing hilarious.

I tried to gulp down some air and give myself a stern talking to. *This is* not *funny. You are an artist. Just blend in.*

Miss Tanner glared at me. Pottery was clearly not a laughing matter for her, but for me that just made the whole thing funnier. I started giggling hard and to my horror the whole class turned to look at me. I needed a way out, something quick to explain the joke – and that joke could absolutely not be Miss Tanner.

"Sorry. I'm laughing because . . . because . . ." I looked across the room, searching for a "thing" that could be the source of laughter. In the corner of my eye a flash of burning orange caught my attention. "Tawny! It was Tawny. She was making me laugh."

I looked at Tawny, whose wide eyes were both confused and flattered at the thought of being funny. Her hands were still thrust above her head. The class was silent as all attention remained on me. Not knowing what else to do, I tried to get everyone back on track with the whole clay-saluting thing. "Going to get back to the clay now," I said awkwardly, my broken voice on the verge of laughing, crying or saying something I would later regret.

Miss Tanner coughed under her breath and a ripple of heads turned their attention back to her. "Okay, voyagers, you know what to do."

And for the rest of the session a group of teenagers held a lump of clay close to their heart, every eye closed as their imaginations danced with form, shape and inspiration.

Eleven

Me: I just had the funniest pottery class

Fidge: Pottery?

Me: Yes, I think I just sold my soul to a lump of clay

Fidge: What?

Me: I wish you were there, it was so intense
Like, in a funny way
The teacher takes her art VERY seriously

Fidge: Pottery?
Pots and stuff?

Me: Yes, turns out Auntie Kate sent me to a different class
Didn't think I could be trusted with Amelie

Fidge: Harsh!

Me: Well I am an attempted murderer so . . .

Fidge: True

Me: Wish you were here. . .
Miss you and Taco
Mostly Taco

Fidge: You okay?

Two bodies bumbled past me and I slipped my phone back into my pocket. "Alpine Adventure" may sound like we were camping in the Alps, but in reality most of the time seemed to be spent weaving around the endless corridors of a prestigious boarding school whose name I could not pronounce, spell or even remember. Pottery class seemed to go on for ever and I was on a mission to simultaneously lose the Ts, who were joining a lunchtime Scrabble tournament, and find Amelie and Ismene. I kept my head down while I tried to figure out where the dining hall was. My stomach was rumbling hard (turns out gloopy tea is not a great start to the day) and I could smell curry. Or was it pizza and fries? Or maybe crepes?

Within minutes I found myself in the heart of the dining hall. I had smelled all of those things and more. There were fresh baguettes filled with cheeses I only ever ate at Amelie's house, a salad bar with food I never knew existed and row after row of warm dishes each smelling of delicious happiness. I was just about to grab a tray and fill it with as many different food options as I could, when a familiar squeal caught my attention. In the far corner of the hall was a swarm of yellow tees hovering around a long wooden table. I knew with confidence who the queen bee of this hive was, only this time I didn't want to murder her. I wanted to give a giant hug to my cousin and sister and tell them all about this weird world I had been thrown into.

I ran as quickly as I could to their table, tripping over bags and bumping into strangers, leaving a trail of chaos behind me and barely noticing.

The second they saw me, Issy and Amelie were on their feet and wrapping their arms around me, their excitement palpable.

"Tig! You're back!" Issy's eyes sparkled with energy and her cheeks were glowing.

"I knew you would find us for lunch. What are you going to eat, Tig? The tacos are *magnifique*!" Amelie sat herself back in the middle of the hive as she waved her arms over the banquet in front of her.

I caught a whiff of one hundred happy smells and made a mental note of the chocolate cake for later. "How's drama class? I wish I was with you."

All eyes were on Amelie as she recounted the morning's session, while my eyes scanned the table to check out her friends. Beautiful people, all of them! They were a group of Amelies, but different styles and nationalities. Every so often Issy would pitch in with some thoughts on Amelie's story, and she looked just as stunning and captivating as the rest of them. I tried to imagine myself in their yellow tee, standing in the middle of the drama studio, performing comedy, improvising new characters, maybe directing a scene or two. It was easy to think of myself at the middle of this dazzling tribe. I was even more of a drama kid than Issy or Amelie. I lived and breathed entertainment and now, in the middle of Switzerland, I had stumbled into my tribe.

My face ached with excitement as I finally understood why this camp was so important to Amelie. Conversations flicked from one person to the next as stories of hilarity and creativity bounced around the table like a balloon at a children's party. All of this in one morning? I could have felt sad to have missed out on the fun, but the enthusiasm of the yellow tees swept me up on a cloud of excitement and I was grateful to finally be with my kind of people.

"So, what does the brown tee mean?"

A quiet fell across the table and I realized that everyone was waiting to hear from me. A girl, around my age, with shimmering brown skin and a mass of glossy curls pouring out of a ponytail on the top of her head, smiled at me curiously. "We are yellow for drama, so what's brown?"

"Oh, I am in pottery class."

Her brow furrowed as the girl with the glossy hair tried to figure out why anyone would want to commit two weeks of their life to pottery.

There was an awkward pause before she tried again: "That's cool. I didn't know there was a pottery option here." She strained her face into a smile as fake grins rippled their way down the table.

I was mortified – I had finally found my people and they all thought I was a clay worshipper like the Ts.

Amelie jumped in and I thought at first it was to my defence, but it seemed not. "So, guys, this is Tig, Ismene's little sister. Tig, this is Madison . . ." Amelie gestured to the girl with the gorgeous ponytail, who flashed me another smile across the table.

"You can call me Maddie."

"And then this is . . ." Amelie began roll-calling all of the yellow tees sitting around the table, but anyone after Maddie was lost on me. I was too busy thinking about how to explain to everyone that I hated pottery and I was actually a drama kid, just like them. I tried to think of the best example I had to illustrate to them all just how passionate I was about drama.

1 I could tell them about my YouTube channel (but they would think I was making unboxing videos or doing the same dance trends everyone does).
2 I could tell them about our home above the Old

Nic (but what if they Googled it and discovered their rehearsal space was more impressive than our professional stage?).

3 I could talk them through Prank Fest (but that could be risky, as I wasn't sure I was ready to tell them all about last summer).

Before I could formulate a response, Ismene jumped to the rescue. "How was pottery class? Was it as boring as it sounds?"

This was the perfect question and I seized the opportunity to demonstrate just how much I was not one of *those* kids. "Boring and weird. We had to salute the clay."

Everyone laughed and I could see an opening for some fun storytelling.

"There is this super-intense teacher, Miss Tanner, who makes you raise your clay above your head like the opening scene of *The Lion King* movie. I swear I almost burst into song."

There was another wave of laughter as one of the yellow tees lifted a water bottle and dramatically sang the opening line. The whole table was laughing and all eyes were on me, so I kept talking.

"It got so weird I couldn't stop giggling and I really offended Miss Tanner. And then there was this thing she makes you do, where you hold the clay to your heart and let it speak to you or something."

Everyone was listening to my story. Even Amelie and Ismene, who seemed just as curious to hear about the strange Miss Tanner. I took them through the different clay activities in our class. I described the other kids with their headphones and long silences. I even had time to introduce the three Ts and the whole "Tony Howl" situation. Each time I thought I should probably hand the conversation to someone else, I would be asked another question and they all listened intently to every word. After a while I felt as though the whole hive was holding on to hear the next story. I felt like the queen bee of the yellow tees, even if I was the only one wearing brown!

The yellow tees had been laughing with me for a while when the energy filtered into the after-laugh – that sweet space where everyone is smiling and a gentle euphoria ebbs through the air like a warm fire on a crispy cold afternoon. I was soaking in the solidarity that always comes from a shared joke when Maddie came at me with another question: "I don't get it. If you hate working with clay so much, why come all this way to do two weeks specializing in pottery?"

All attention was still on me and without even thinking I blurted out, "Ugh, it's my auntie Kate's way of punishing me. Think Wicked Witch of the West meets Lord Farquaad and that is my delightful aunt." I laughed at my own joke, confident that everyone else would too, but a hush fell across the hive. Disappointed by their reaction I threw in another joke: "My auntie Kate is so over the top she makes a thunderstorm out of a rain shower."

Again, there was no laughter, not even a smile, in fact. How had I lost them so quickly? I decided to try one more. . . "If it was just the two of us left on earth I would sooner live alone in the middle of the Arctic Circle and risk being mauled by a polar bear than spend an evening with cruel Kate."

Maddie was shocked – the whole hive was. "We have known Kate for years. She doesn't seem like that."

A huge lump formed in my throat. I hadn't thought they might actually know Kate, but then of course they would – she was Amelie's *mother*! I looked across to Amelie as my face turned a pale yellow. I hadn't meant to humiliate Amelie. I hadn't even been thinking of Amelie.

My cousin's face was red and her jaw was locked shut. She was raging. Quietly, sure, but raging nonetheless. I wanted to say something that would smooth the whole thing over, but my mind was like a boat wedged onto the shore, refusing to move anywhere.

Ismene cut in and I prayed that she would find just the right thing to say. "She is nice. Tig is just joking."

"So why is she forcing Tig to make pottery?" another yellow tee chimed in, but I couldn't even look up to see who it was.

Ismene continued, desperately trying to tidy up my mess, again. "It's just Auntie Kate thought Antigone would enjoy a change of hobbies and . . . also she . . . erm . . ."

Ismene was losing it and I thought things were about to erupt, when Amelie jumped in. "Tig is super-cute, my *maman* loves her – we all do. But she's also, you know, more contained in the pottery room, less likely to cause damage!"

Amelie let out a hearty, sparkly eyed laugh that showed all her teeth and ricocheted throughout the hive. She was mocking me. But I was mocking her mother. This was a terrible situation to be in.

I opened my mouth to say something that would make Amelie's summary of me less socially damaging, but Ismene was having none of it.

"I can't believe it. Next session starts in twenty minutes. We had better get back to the drama studio." Ismene stood with so much authority and determination that the rest of the hive followed her in gathering their things. She kept talking. For Ismene, she was talking a lot. "We need to get going, but you enjoy the food, Antigone, and make something pretty in pottery, a nice jug or something . . . a pot, maybe?"

Her last words trailed behind her as a mass of yellow tees began weaving their way through the dining hall. I looked up in time to see Amelie give me a stern sideways stare before joining the rest of the hive buzzing back to the drama studio.

Twelve

My phone buzzed in my pocket.

FIDGE: You okay?

I knew exactly how to answer: I was categorically *not* okay! I had finally met a bunch of people who I knew would totally get me, and instead of hanging out with them I was stuck with some weird girls who were obsessed with worshipping clay and anything beginning with the letter T! The people I wanted to love me thought I had problems with behaving myself and that I needed "containing", and the people I didn't want to hang out with were *everywhere*!

I was just about to text my long rant into my phone when a voice spoke gently behind me: "That is quite a lot of food for one person."

I span around and was confronted by a bright yellow tee, another one. My mind was too occupied with the social injustices of Alpine Adventure to register any more than "boy in a yellow tee". I muttered back, "It's not my food."

"Yeah, I guessed. Care to share?"

My fingers drummed furiously over the letters on my phone as I mumbled my reply: "Sure."

There was quiet as I poured my heart into my message to Fidge, explaining the horror of being a girl like me in a place like this. I sensed the boy sit down across the table and begin to nibble on some cucumber and humous.

"Kim."

I looked up. "Pardon?"

"I am Kim, and you are . . .?"

"Oh, I am Antigone."

"Hello, Antigone."

The boy smiled at me from across the table and I tried to adjust myself back into being kind, sociable Tig. "Yes, hi!" Kim was smiling warmly at me, knowingly, which was strange since we had only just met. I could see he was expecting me to speak, so I tried my best: "You're a yellow tee, so that's drama class, right?" I pretended it was all new to me.

"Right, and you are brown, so . . . pottery?"

I nodded as my cheeks flushed pink. I was still reeling from the last conversation and couldn't muster the strength for round two. Kim was still staring at me, his dewy skin, dark eyelashes and silky hair making him look as though he had fallen straight out of a K-pop music video. I looked away, pretending I hadn't noticed his resemblance to pop royalty and grabbed a chunk of dry bread before attempting to chew the end off. The bread was hard and clearly meant to be soaked in the delicious vegetable broth it was sitting next to. I looked over at Kim, who was still smiling, still watching me. I had two choices: spit the bread out and admit that I had no clue about the food or the table or why I was even here, or keep being awkward with a huge chunk of dry bread stuck between my teeth. Aunt Kate's reprimand rattled around my head: *Swiss customs around cuisine are even more defined than the French.*

It was an easy decision. I kept chomping and sucking that bread, hoping it would shrink. Any normal human would have given up and found another more normal person to chat with, but not Kim. He was looking at me as if I was someone he had been hoping to meet. Had I not been eating a giant piece of dry bread I would have managed the situation expertly, but you know bread!

"I never thought Antigone Kingsley would be sat on her own." His eyes were locked onto mine. I couldn't speak, but my face did not hide my surprise. Kim carried on, "I never thought Antigone Kingsley would be doing pottery, either."

My neck was hot, my heart was pounding, my hands were clammy. Surely the yellow tees hadn't managed to tell everyone about my disastrous introduction already? The bread had softened into a soggy ball and I swallowed it down in one big gulp.

"I was kind of disappointed to see you in a brown shirt. I had hoped you would be in yellow."

My mind was split in two. Was Kim horribly creepy, or kind of enchanting?

"Do I know you?" I asked, smoothing down my hair and straightening my back.

"No, but I know you. JustTigging, right?"

JustTigging, my YouTube channel! I breathed out a sigh of relief. He wasn't a crazy guy; he was a fan!

"Right, sure, that's me!"

"Thought so!"

There was a pause. My phone lit up. I glanced at it and realized I had left Fidge on "typing". I deleted my draft message and slipped my phone to the side, allowing my full attention to land on this curious K-pop lookalike sitting opposite me. I had never been in this situation before, and struggled to think of a way to talk to my YouTube audience without saying "Hi guys. . ." first. But Kim was a social pro. He didn't need me to carry the conversation; he didn't need anything.

"So, Antigone . . . or can I call you Tig?"

"You can," I said casually.

"Tig, how are you finding pottery class?"

My stomach rolled over at the humiliation of being a drama girl trapped in a pottery girl's tee. "It was *not* my choice to go. There was a mix-up."

"Can't you straighten it out? I'm sure we can make space for you in the drama class. My dad virtually paid for the entire studio. I can pull some strings and have you moved across?"

I fought the urge to shout, *That would be AMAZING! Let's do it now!* Even my impulsivity knows you don't take on Auntie Kate. When she puts you somewhere you stay put!

"I think I am better off where I am."

"Making pots? Come on, Antigone Kingsley, where's your sense of adventure? Join me in drama. We will have so much fun. You can teach me some pranks."

"I can't. It's complicated, but my aunt wants me to do pottery." I hated every word I spoke. Kim was showering me in smiles and attention, and all I could do was shrink inside my dull brown T-shirt.

"Don't tell me. Crazy Kate thinks you are going to take Amelie down again?"

A blade of invisible ice ran through my body and shattered me into tiny pieces. My jaw dropped open wide and my head span. "How do you know? Who told . . . What?"

I know myself well enough to know my hair was frizzing up to the size and texture of a haystack with the amount of heat steaming off the back of my neck. My face prickled red and my jaw had been open for a while, but still Kim looked at me as though I was exquisitely beautiful.

I coughed and pulled myself together before announcing firmly, "I'm sorry. I don't know what you're referring to."

"I started following you when Amelie was on your prank hit list. Our families have known each other for years." His words were smooth and unfazed by my awkwardness. "When I saw you take Amelie on, I was impressed. Not many people take on the queen!"

"It was a misunderstanding that got out of hand." My answer was quick and defensive.

There was a pause as Kim studied my response, his eyes rolling over my face thoughtfully. "Well, I am glad you're here, Antigone Kingsley, even if you *are* stuck in the pottery room."

Through flustered cheeks and sweaty hair, I managed to give him a smile of gratitude.

"I am going back to drama now, so see you tomorrow for lunch?"

I nodded again. Kim began heading for the same exit the rest of his hive had taken just moments earlier as he made his way through the crowds and towards the drama studio. Seconds before leaving the hall he called out, "See you tomorrow, Antigone Kingsley. It's a date!"

A wave of heads turned towards me, curious as to who this Antigone Kingsley was and why she was going on a "date" with K-pop Kim. My heart thumped furiously in my chest as a spark of embarrassment already forming in my stomach burst into a full-blown furnace, turning every inch of my skin vibrant red.

I sank my head into my chest and pretended to be busy on my phone until everyone lost interest.

FIDGE: Tig? You okay?
ME: Yes, all good

Thirteen

"Alpine is buzzing and it's incredible to be here in Switzerland . . ."

Tawny was in shot again. I had been trying to make a YouTube video for over an hour and no matter where I went in the room, Tawny's orange glow appeared in the corner of the shot. Ideally I would have filmed with a backdrop of giant mountains and vibrant lakes, but it seemed Alpine was more of an indoor adventure place.

"Tawny, why don't you sit here, behind the camera?" It wasn't the first time I had asked her. Tawny was stealthy and could move silently across the room, and even when she promised to keep out of the frame, she would be there moments later, a big smile plastered across her face. I was ready to try for the hundredth time, when the dorm room door was thrust open by an exuberant Talia.

"I've just been to the office. Teresa has sent us a sleepover party pack! Look, we have a chess board, Monopoly and a new strategy game that is really very hard and you have to focus so, so much. Which shall we play first?"

Both girls were jumping up and down with excitement. Board games are my worst nightmare. You have to sit indoors remembering pointless rules, being told what to do before losing or, most of the time, giving up.

"Come on, Tiggy Tig Tig, you can be the games master." Talia passed me the rule book and a little groan slipped out of my mouth. I put my phone away, the YouTube video was clearly not happening. "Oh and also, Tiggy Tig Tig, Jada is waiting to see you in the hall."

I was so relieved for the excuse to exit, I threw the rules on the bed and darted to the hall. Jada smiled as she opened her arms to offer a hug and, deciding she was my favourite human at Alpine, I gladly received.

"How are you settling in, sweetie?"

The cuddle, the smooth American accent, the sympathetic eyes. I replied without thinking, "I hate it."

Jada seemed concerned as she gently rubbed her hand up and down my back just like my mum would. "Sweetie, I'm so sorry to hear that."

"I hate pottery, I hate being a T, I hate stupid board games, I hate Tiggy Tig Tig."

Jada was full of compassion but her lips were smiling and she giggled as she spoke. "Tiggy Tig Tig?"

"It's what Talia and Tawny call me. They think we're five years old. Please, Jada, you *have* to get me out of here. Let me go to drama class, or send me home. Either is fine, just don't leave me here!"

Jada seemed conflicted and for a tiny second I thought there may be some hope, but then she said, "I can't do that, sweetie." I breathed out a miserable sigh as she continued, "Why don't you give things a chance? Okay, so pottery isn't your thing, but Talia and Tawny are the kindest girls on campus . . . and so are *you*. Why don't you introduce them to some of the things you enjoy?"

She was probably right. And I kinda liked her. And she was stroking my back. I nodded and pulled my shoulders back a little.

"So, what would you normally do on a sleepover?" she asked.

My mind flashed back to a few nights earlier, when I was crying in the spare room at Auntie Kate's house. I shrugged.

"Let's see, when I was your age my sister and I did face packs, we made up dances, watched movies, had pillow fights . . . Any of those your thing?"

Actually, that all sounded totally my thing. Normally it would take a while to break a bad mood, but Jada's words swept through me like a cool breeze.

"Yeah, I can do that. Or pranks?"

"Pranks?" Jada laughed. "Okay, but maybe leave those for tomorrow night."

I giggled, imagining how easy it would be to prank the Ts.

"You be you, Antigone, that's all."

I smiled and went in for a side hug. "Thank you."

Jada was right. I needed to give Talia and Tawny a chance. I needed to give myself a chance. I took a deep breath and went back into the dorm as Jada called behind me, "Go get 'em, Tiggy Tig Tig!"

Talia was reading a long list of rules aloud as Tawny delicately set up a complex system of cards and characters on a complicated board.

"So, Tiggy Tig Tig is yellow, and she can swipe, switch, drop or dart when she moves horizontally to Tony, who is pink. But Tony can only twist, rise, fight or shimmy if she is point two to the left of . . ."

Okay, to be honest I'm making this bit up, but board-game rules hurt my brain and I didn't listen beyond "So . . .". Whatever strategy Talia was trying to explain, I quickly diverted attention to another idea.

"Okay, girls, Teresa's game sounds awesome, but tonight I have another idea."

They both looked at me with hopeful eyes. I had no idea if they were ready for this, but I yelled at the top of my voice, "PILLOW FIGGGGHHHHTTTT!"

I grabbed a pillow from Tawny's bed and swiped it across the bottom of her legs, causing Tawny to scream, grab a pillow and come back for revenge. She thrust the pillow across my face before knocking Talia across the back. But Talia was ready. Talia was born ready. Armed with a pillow in either hand she spun them both around like helicopter blades, taking out me, Tawny and everything else in her path. Game characters, soft toys, brown tees and paper flew everywhere. There was a loud pop as a packet of snacks burst open, but it didn't stop us. We swung our pillows in every direction, screaming and laughing till our tummies ached. I was buzzing and my head pounded with excitement as every little piece of me felt wide awake. I was seeing these crazy Ts go from focused board gamers to hard-core pillow fighters in no time at all.

We fought a good fight until our fingers struggled to clasp the pillows. There was a moment of quiet, and I assumed it was a natural end to the battle. I was a little disappointed, and ready for more as always, but they had given me a good run. Talia threw herself backwards onto her bed and let out an exhausted giggle. So I joined her, sinking my head into a pile of soft toys and cards. My face was smiling and my muscles trembling, but my brain felt beautifully still.

All of a sudden there was a bloodcurdling yell as Tawny sprung from a crouching position onto the bed, landing like a ninja before hammering Talia with strike after strike of pillowy squishiness. Seeing tiny Tawny transform into the Incredible Hulk was so funny I howled with laughter until tears fell down my face and I could barely breathe. Then, seizing the moment to take her down, I wrapped my hands around her little ankles and swiped her feet from underneath her.

There was quiet. A horrible, stinging silence as Tawny crumpled like a piece of tissue paper and fell backwards off the bed. I closed my eyes in terror, hoping I could vanish from the room, but all I could see was her little body . . . no, Amelie's . . . no, Tawny's . . . both of them hitting the ground with a deafening thud.

I hid my face and covered my ears as Talia called out, "Tony, are you okay?"

I held my breath. I wanted to leave camp, but not like this – not as an attempted murd—

"You can't defeat me that easily, Tiggy Tig Tig!"

A triumphant Tawny rose from the ashes, her hands wielding two pillows and her face smeared in blood and vengeance. She was the strangest girl I had ever met.

Fourteen

Waking up on day two at Alpine, I knew exactly who was sitting on my feet. I opened my eyes to Tawny holding out a green mug of tea. She still had the bright orange halo of morning hair sticking out in every direction, but this time a long piece of tissue trailed from either nostril, each with little polka dots of dried blood splattered along it.

"Tawny, is your nose still bleeding?" I shuddered, hoping our minor incident wasn't a big one after all.

"Oh no, Tiggy Tig Tig. I have a little scratch and I can't stop picking at it, that's all. You want your tea? It is only a little bit cold today." She pushed the mug further towards me. Tawny was so delighted to be needed that I gratefully received her gift and took it straight into the bathroom, locking the door before pouring the gloopy drink down the sink. I looked in the mirror and noticed a splurge of dried blood on my nose. I wiped it away and the lack of broken skin confirmed it was Tawny's. I giggled to myself in the mirror and secretly wished I had brought the portrait of JC from my bedroom to have a little chat with. The image of Jesus Christ had once been a print on a discarded prop under the Old Nic stage, but since moving the picture to my bedroom last summer, JC had become my no-judgement listening post.

I quickly readied myself for the day, but before leaving the bathroom, I called out to JC, ready to speak to the painting like I would back home. You know, just in case. . . "Hey JC, those two are hilarious! I thought I broke Tawny, but she seems to be made of steel. And Talia, she is all rules and routines one minute and then raging bull the next (in a fun way). And there is this kid called Kim. He . . ." I watched as my cheeks flushed pink in the mirror. "Anyway, pottery aside, it turns out Alpine might actually be okay!"

Talia and Tawny were waiting by the door by the time I had finished getting ready. We walked through the halls of Alpine, which were slowly becoming familiar, and Talia talked the whole way as Tawny ran alongside us on her tippy toes, trying to keep up. It was too soon to be considered friends, but walking into the art studio with a T on either side definitely made me feel less alone.

Miss Tanner, however, was still as intense as the day before.

"As apprentices of clay, you must consider this warm ball in your hand as a teacher, friend, servant and guide. Now again, students, you know what to do . . ."

I lifted the ball of clay into the air as Talia whispered into my ear, "Learning fast, Tiggy Tig Tig!" She was smiling cheekily and I wasn't sure if she was complimenting me in earnest or sharing a joke. Either way I giggled back.

Miss Tanner continued her long speech about shape and beauty and power and fried fish. (I possibly misheard that bit or zoned out.) Every word was spoken with passion and sincerity. She finished with, "Go! But do not speak. Just go."

All around me students lowered their hands and began shuffling around the room with balls of clay. Realizing I had missed an important part of Miss Tanner's speech I called across to Tawny, "What are we supposed to be doing?"

But Tawny was already too engrossed in a pile of old newspapers to hear me.

I tried again: "What are we suppo—"

"Antigone Kingsley, I said do *not* speak." Miss Tanner glared at me from behind her purple glasses.

"Sorry, Miss, I am not sure what—"

"That is called *speaking*, Antigone Kingsley. *Do not speak.*"

I paused on the spot, looking around to see if I could work out what task everyone was fulfilling. There was a kid rolling clay on the floor, someone sticking clay to their shoe, while another student was moulding the ball into a duck shape, or possibly a car. Unable to figure out what on earth we had been asked to do, I decided to try Miss Tanner again. "Sorry, Miss, what are we—"

She interrupted me by snapping her fingers in front of my face before motioning a zipping sign across her lips, locking the imaginary zip, and hiding an imaginary key in her pocket. I couldn't believe I'd thought she was going to be cool. I considered turning away to give myself some more time to figure out what everyone was up to, but Miss Tanner stepped even closer, her beady eyes daring me to take her on. I was completely confused and my cheeks were becoming redder by the second. No one wants to be the "stuck" one in any classroom, but when it's an abstract art class at an elite boarding school in one of the top educational institutions in the world, it feels crushingly worse.

Just then Talia came over to Miss Tanner, her eyes dancing with excitement as she showed our teacher the clay, moulded into a triangle. I stared at the clay, I stared at Talia. I still had no idea what was happening. But then neither did Miss Tanner, it seemed. She studied the triangle in awe, clearly trying to comprehend the wonder of this magnificent three-sided shape.

Talia pulled Miss Tanner's attention towards the other side of the room, giving Tawny time to sweep in and drop a note in my hand saying, "For the next two weeks, we have to create something that means 'harmony'. You can do anything, Tiggy Tig Tig; it's art!"

I crumpled the piece of paper into a ball and shoved it in my pocket before Miss Tanner could catch me receiving help.

Harmony. Okay, I can do this. Just think what Mum would do.

Miss Tanner kept her sharp stare on me for the rest of the session, but I wasn't too bothered. For three hours it was just me and my imagination, pressing, rolling and shaping the clay into the beginnings of a gloriously tall tree that would house three small wise owls.

Fifteen

"You *have* to come to Scrabble club, Tiggy Tig Tig. Yesterday Tony got a word with very many letters and it was just so funny. We really really laughed, didn't we, Tony?"

As much as I enjoyed the pillow fighting and appreciated the heads-up in pottery class, I was not so loyal to my new friends that Scrabble club could be an option. Besides, I had a date with K-pop Kim. I mean, not a *date* date. It was a hang-out, over lunch, in a canteen. It was no big deal!

"It's okay – you two go to Scrabble. I promised to meet Issy and Amelie for lunch."

A shadow formed on Tawny's face as she leaned closely towards Talia. "Perhaps we should go with Tiggy Tig Tig and meet her family?"

"No!" I blurted out a little too forcefully. "No, you guys go to Scrabble club. I don't want you to miss out." I could not allow myself to be Tiggy Tig Tig in front of K-pop Kim and the yellow tees. I would not let it happen.

"*Madre Mia*, Tawny is right. I am so rude." Talia looked mortified with herself. "Of course we will come with you and meet your family."

I shuffled uncomfortably, trying to formulate a solid excuse. "That's probably . . . I mean . . . you have Scrabble, you know? There are all those letters . . ."

They both looked at me with such dedication I knew it would take an earthquake to shake them off.

"Antigone Kingsley!" Suddenly my name was called from down the hall. "There you are. I thought you had stood me up!" Kim's whole face was lit up like the midday sun and all his light was blazing down on me.

"Excuse me, ladies. I need to borrow your friend. We have a date."

Tawny and Talia looked over at me, their mouths wide open. They were shocked about the date, they were shocked about the lie. I knew what was coming next.

"But Tiggy Tig Tig. I thought you said—"

"Yes, that's right. We can catch up after lunch. Enjoy Scrabble!"

I walked away as quickly as I could, still trying to decide which scandal was worse: being called Tiggy Tig Tig in front of K-pop Kim or lying about a date or even going on a date – I mean, I was thirteen. I didn't *date.* No one in Brinstock Academy goes on a "lunch date" at school. What world was I living in?

I tried to reason with myself. *I did lie a little bit, but I* am *hanging out with the yellow tees, so technically*

Amelie and Ismene are probably going to be there. And also . . . this isn't a date!

I stormed through the halls not even noticing where I was going or that K-pop Kim was running behind me trying to keep up. I stopped suddenly, in the middle of the entrance hall, the same spot where Jada had taken me to just two days earlier when she revealed Aunt Kate's sinister plan.

Kim came bounding up behind me, his smile still radiating in my direction. "Hey, Tiggy Tig Tig . . ."

"Please don't call me that—"

"What's got you running through the corridors so fast? Are you trying to lose me?" I could tell by the glimmer of confidence in his eyes that Kim would never believe that someone didn't want to hang out with him.

"Sorry, I'm just really hungry. Which way is it to the canteen again?"

Kim held up two large brown bags, each filled to the brim with delicious food. "No need. I've got everything here."

It was a relief being with someone who was in charge for a change and as we nestled into the grassy mounds down by the river, I felt myself begin to relax. Kim chatted endlessly about his world as he piled up an extraordinary amount of food – enough to cater for all of the yellow tees and more! I glanced at my watch and wondered when the others would be arriving. It was already one o'clock; lunch break would be over soon. I took in a deep breath and enjoyed the sensation of cool air running into my chest. The skies were a vibrant blue and the clouds were so fluffy it was as though they had been carefully crafted that way.

"How are you finding Switzerland?" Kim laid back into the grass as he twirled a carrot stick through his fingers.

"This is the first time I have been outside."

He laughed out loud before looking at me in shock. "Are you being serious?"

"Yes! I thought I was going to be dancing through the Alps singing 'do rei mi', not stuck inside playing Scrabble and bonding with clay."

Kim was smiling as he waited for me to explain some more.

"If I had known it would be like this I would have stayed at home."

"With Taco and Fidge, right?"

My heart did a little leap inside. I had forgotten how much I'd shared online. It never occurred to me that anyone was actually paying attention. "Yeah, I guess," I said dismissively as I pulled my hair forward to cover my blushing cheeks. Kim seemed not to notice.

"You're not really getting the whole Alpine experience. Those girls you are sharing a room with are weird."

I laughed, remembering Tawny leaping like Hulk onto my bed. "Yes! 'Quirky', my mum would say. I have never met anyone like them."

"They are the boring kids. No one bothers learning their names because we know we will never need to use them."

Kim sounded a bit harsh. They weren't *that* bad. But honestly, the open sky and clear running river in front of me was so perfect, I didn't see the need to ruin it by jumping to the Ts' defence.

"How did you end up getting stuck with them anyway? Amelie's mum must really hate you."

I smiled awkwardly. There was a little bee bouncing from flower to flower in a bundle of wild pink and purple thistles. I watched as it hovered delicately before stopping for a rest on the tip of my foot.

Kim was still talking. "I wouldn't worry about your aunt. Amelie always gets treated like a princess. It is not your fault." Kim watched me watching the bee. "So, you're an outdoors girl then?"

I took a deep breath and allowed the sun to sprinkle across my eyelids. "Yes, I love it. Everything feels better outside."

"You're going to love the last day of camp then. They have told you about hike day, right?"

I shook my head, vaguely remembering my mum reading about a trophy on the website.

"Every year teams take to the mountain for a six-hour hike. It is a tradition that spans generations at the end of the school year, and it was such a success that the teachers in charge of summer camp decided to copy. For one day the whole camp turns feverish with excitement: matching costumes, chanting, energy food, music; it's like a carnival and an Olympic event in one. No teachers, no adults – just you and your team in the big outdoors. And the winners take the trophy!"

I let out a sigh of contentment. "Finally, something to look forward to!"

Kim laughed and threw his head back as light shone through his glossy hair. "You don't have to be stuck with the weirdos either. You can join my team. One call from my dad and I can get you moved across to drama."

Kim seemed kind and concerned and completely on my side. It was tempting to use his influence and sidle across to drama. I tried to imagine Kate's reaction. Maybe she would go crazy at first, but maybe, just maybe, it would teach her a lesson. She could try and wreck my life, but she would never win.

Kim looked at me pleadingly and I knew he would do his very best to help me.

"I can't. It isn't worth the backlash. I *love* drama, but only on stage. Kate will create chaos and I don't have the energy for that."

"Well, if you change your mind let me know. It's just a phone call, that is all."

We stayed together chatting and soaking up the sunshine for a whole hour. No one else from the yellow tees arrived and I was surprised to see that neither Amelie nor Ismene had bothered to message me and say they weren't coming. I mean, it was lunch break, and everyone hangs out with their teams at lunch, right? And Kim had gone to so much trouble to bring all of the food. I was a little annoyed with them both, but not enough to ruin a perfect hour.

Sixteen

The lovely thing about Talia and Tawny was that they had zero expectations of me. I had prepared myself for a tough conversation about dumping Scrabble for Kim and lying about meeting Amelie and Ismene, but neither of them seemed betrayed or even very bothered. The frustrating thing about Talia and Tawny was how they had zero understanding of personal space.

As soon as pottery class was over (my tree was coming together and actually looked pretty amazing) I headed outside to look for more pretty places, with a bubbling idea for a new YouTube video I wanted to film. I spotted a gentle glow of sunlight sparkling over the river, and a rock sitting under a shimmy of light, surrounded by pink and purple wildflowers. It was the ideal place. I made myself comfortable and got to work.

"Hey guys. It has been a while since my last video. Alpine Adventure has been keeping me pretty busy . . ." I paused. There was a flash of orange in the corner of the screen. Tawny! I looked around and waited for a few moments, but there was nothing there – just the cool greens and warm hues of Switzerland at golden hour. I moved on with my video.

"So, let me tell you about Alpine. This place is . . ." It was there again. I spun around and scoured the area with my eyes. Still nothing. Was I being paranoid?

I tried again: "So, let me tell you about Alpine. This place is . . ." And there she was. Hiding behind the bushes, her orange hair gleaming through the green leaves.

"Tawny, I can see you!" A huge giggle bellowed out from behind the bushes and I knew at once that Tawny had not come alone. "Talia, I can hear you!"

The Ts tumbled out from behind the bushes with raucous belly laughs.

"I'm sorry, Tiggy Tig Tig." Tawny looked a little forlorn, but I knew she would do the same thing again.

Talia, however, was showing no repentance. "Come on, Tiggy Tig Tig. Teresa showed us your channel; it is so funny. Please, you have to let us be on it!"

They sat themselves at my feet as Talia begged some more: "You know, very many people say I am so funny, and look at Tony – she is made for comedy!"

Tawny cupped her hands under her chin to emphasize her cheeky smile before adding: "Put us in your video, Tiggy Tig Tig. *Please!*"

I watched them both pull at my feet to aid their melodramatic begging. I thought about it. They were actually pretty funny when you got to know them, and Scrabble aside they could be fun. But one little comment from Kim kept niggling at me: *They are the boring kids. No one bothers learning their names because we know we will never need to use them.* What if it was true? What if putting them on my channel made people hate them? What if it bored my audience away? What if it made me look boring too? It was too much of a risk for all of us.

"I can't. It's not that kind of channel."

I put my phone into my pocket and made my way back to the dorm.

Seventeen

Me: What are you up to?
Fidge: Playing cards with Taco
I'm winning
You?
Me: Sitting on my bed
Fidge: Alpine sounds adventurous
Me: Yep . . .
I think I upset my roommates
Fidge: How?
Me: They want to be on my YouTube
And I can't let them
Fidge: Why not?
Me: Cause they're . . . different
Fidge: ???

Tawny and Talia had still not come back to the room. It was dark outside and the phone light blared into my eyes.

Me: They're really nice and I find them funny, but they're odd
Fidge: How?

ME:	Well, my friend said they are so boring no one even bothers learning their names
FIDGE:	Nice friend. Which one?
ME:	. . . Kim
FIDGE:	Is she from Ismene and Amelie's dorm room?

I stared at the phone for a few seconds, running the possible replies through my mind.

ME:	Kim is in Amelie and Ismene's drama class
FIDGE:	How weird can they be?
ME:	Tawny is like "Where's Wally?" Every time I make a video she's hiding in the picture somewhere
FIDGE:	Waldo
ME:	Huh?
FIDGE:	Where's Waldo? . . .for your new international friends . . . sounds like a hilarious YouTube video and definitely not boring. Ditch Kim, she sounds mean

The bedroom door creaked open as Tawny and Talia crept sheepishly into the room.

"Can we come in, Tiggy Tig Tig?"

I leaned across to the bedside table and switched on the lamp. "Of course you can."

They both looked sullen and thoroughly ashamed of themselves. Talia took a deep breath and stepped a little closer to me. "Tiggy Tig Tig, Tony and I have spoken to Teresa and she explain me that YouTube is very many work and it is understandable that you would not want to be reckless with your content."

Tawny looked as though she was about to burst into tears as her thin voice whispered out, "I have been very unfair to you. I won't do that again."

I couldn't believe *they* were apologizing to *me*. Kim was right, they were odd, but then maybe odd could be a good thing? I looked at them both, huddled together with their heads hung low in shame. My heart melted into a pile of sticky toffee and I couldn't help but run over and give them both a huge hug. "No, I'm sorry. It was rude of me. I shouldn't have stormed off. And anyway, you're right. You two are hilarious."

They both looked at me sceptically.

"You are! In fact, I was just speaking with my co-producer, and we have had a great idea for a new video. Have you guys heard of 'Where's Waldo?'?"

It was amazing how easy it was to find a red-and-white striped bobble hat and sweater. As soon as

Tawny managed to squash all of her hair into the hat, we set to work framing shots for me to speak, while Tawny, or Waldo rather, found a weird place to hide. I did an empty canteen with Waldo blending into a menu board, and in the garden with Waldo behind the bushes. We even managed to get Waldo peering out of a pile of recycling.

While all other Alpine adventurers were sleeping in their beds, me and the Ts were running around the empty halls of Alpine Adventure Youth Camp making JustTigging episode 93, "Where's Waldo?!"

Fidge was a genius. His idea worked better than I could have hoped and was loads better than my boring catch-up vlog by the river. Kim would love it. I was sure he would.

Eighteen

Pottery class seemed over in a second. I finished my tree and it looked reasonable, but then Miss Tanner showed me a technique for adding texture and I couldn't believe how good it looked. I was just about to start working on my owls when the lunch bell rang, and there was somewhere I needed to be. I ran to the drama studio with two large bags of muffins, sandwiches and fruit that I had managed to grab from the canteen after breakfast.

My plan was to have lunch outside with Ismene and Amelie, but I was definitely on the look-out for Kim and the rest of the yellow tees too. It was cool having my pottery crew, but you can never have too many friends.

I peered through the drama window and at once a flurry of excitement rose up in my chest. There was an entire wall filled floor to ceiling with extravagant costumes. There were large prop boxes underneath, with various labels like "kitchen", "hats and bags" and "weaponry". I needed to be in that room!

In the corner I could see Maddie, her long hair falling over someone as she applied their make-up.

She adjusted her position and I caught a glimpse of Amelie having a fake nose put on. I laughed, remembering how much Amelie had mocked me for the SFX-wearing, but quickly softened my thoughts towards her. We had made friends, right? But then there was the whole me mocking her mother and her giving me the side-eye thing . . . I darted out of Amelie's sight line, just in case.

Ismene was dressed in a long white robe, with her hair tumbling down her back as she recited lines from a script and marched up and down a small stage. She seemed so at home and I desperately wanted to run in and join her. That was the plan, after all: to take them for a riverside lunch, just as Kim and I had enjoyed the day before. But seeing them all so engrossed in their work and clearly not rushing for lunch made me feel a bit desperate.

"Looking for someone?"

I felt a whisper in the back of my neck. I jumped around in shock to see Kim, laughing warmly.

"Good to see you hanging around the drama studio, Tiggy Tig Tig. Does this mean you have come to your senses and are joining team yellow?" Kim had only been in my world for a few days, but the sound of his voice already felt like the start of an adventure.

"I come bearing gifts. Well, lunch actually. I thought I would see if you guys wanted to come to the river?" I glanced back through the window to see if Ismene and Amelie looked close to finishing. They clearly weren't.

Kim looked at me empathetically. "I think they are going to be a while. They are rehearsing for a performance this afternoon." His eyes were warm and gentle, as though he understood how hard it was for me to be there at Alpine but not *there* in drama.

I pulled away from the window, suddenly feeling a bit ridiculous about my lunch plans. "Yeah, sure, no, that's fine. I should probably get back to pottery anyway, so . . ." I backed away from the door, ready to go and find a hole to hide away in, but Kim pulled my hand gently back.

"I'm free. We could hang out together again if you want?"

My cheeks surged a vibrant red, as they did so often when Kim was around. "Sounds good." I shrugged casually.

Another hour spent by the river was exactly what I needed. We ate our lunch barefoot, with cool water washing over our toes. I wanted to know everything about the drama studio world and Kim didn't hold back on any information, talking freely about the exercises, the crazy improvisations and the politics of who always landed the lead role and who always fell to the sidelines. He told me the highs, lows and friendship drama of the yellow tees I had met briefly in the canteen. I found out that Maddie had stopped boarding at the school a few years earlier, after her dad made some bad investments, but her grandmother ensured she could still make it to camp each year with generous donations. I discovered that this kid called Louis was fourth in line to a hotel dynasty that had begun with a small boutique in Italy and grown to one of the largest, longest-serving hotel chains in America, and that his uncle was currently putting the whole family's wealth on the line with his penchant for the party life. And then Aurelia, who I couldn't actually picture and I had no idea if we had even met, well, she and Kim had once been really close friends, but when Amelie joined the camp she and Aurelia teamed up and were so mean to Kim he actually thought about quitting drama altogether. I was embarrassed to think of Amelie behaving that way, given that we were family, but it didn't really surprise me.

I listened, completely intrigued. These kids had the kind of lives my parents would put on the stage at the Old Nic, weaving their complicated plot lines in and out of each other. Real drama like this never happened in Brinstock! We never knew what people owned or earned or inherited. We just assumed it wasn't very much, like the rest of us. And the more I listened, the easier Kim found it to share everything. I felt privileged to hear him speak so openly about his friends and family, and I was incredibly grateful to have found a friendship within the first few days of camp. Especially with someone who looked like a popstar.

It was getting late. I mean, it *was* late. I looked at my watch and lunch had been over for at least an hour. Kim didn't seem in a rush to move and since he knew better than me how things worked at Alpine, I couldn't really see the point in hurrying back to my tree and owls. They were looking good, but clay could wait.

"I am so glad you came to camp, Antigone. Thanks for the lunch."

I smiled warmly at him. "No, I have to thank *you*! I could have been sat on my own at lunch or, worse, in Scrabble club." I laughed as a cosy sensation ran through my body. It was true, Kate had set me up for the worst time, but finding Kim was actually kind of wonderful.

"You know, it isn't too late to jump across to drama?" Kim winked at me playfully, knowing I wouldn't agree.

"I can't. And anyway, drama sounds kind of intense. I think I prefer playing Wally with the Ts."

"Playing what?"

For a moment I forgot Kim's comments about Talia and Tawny as memories of the three of us making videos in the sleeping halls of Alpine filled me with enthusiasm. "You know the kids' books, 'Where's Wally?', or Waldo I think you guys call him? Stripey hat, stripey sweater?"

"Yeah, I know the guy."

"Well, Talia, Tawny and I are making our own version for my YouTube channel, only Tawny is Waldo. It's super-funny – well, it will be when we finish filming."

Kim pulled his feet out of the water, swivelling himself round before standing up. "That's so nice of you, Antigone. You're so kind like that."

I swivelled myself up too, and began drying my feet off. I smiled smugly to myself at the mention of me being "nice". It was a lot better than "chaotic" or "problematic", or whatever other things Aunt Kate had said about me. I had tried hard to find friendship with the Ts, and Kim could clearly see that. I smiled at him, feeling proud of myself and pleased he could spot my good bits.

Kim reached out a hand and placed it warmly on my shoulder. "You know you shouldn't post it though, right? Those girls are not the vibe you want on your channel. They're far too dull for JustTigging."

There was a pause. I looked into Kim's warm eyes and felt his concern for me. But still, there was a little knot forming in my chest, and it usually only came out when something wasn't quite right. I smiled at Kim, not sure what to say, but he seemed to take it as full confirmation that I would do as he asked.

"Good! Not that you need me to tell you that – you live with them. You know how weird they are."

I mean, he had a point. But who says weird is a *bad* thing? My voice shook a little as I spoke. "Yeah, I get it."

But Kim never noticed. He was on to the next thing already. "I need you to understand that *you* are my favourite thing about Alpine Adventure, so promise me one thing?"

All bad thoughts sloughed from my mind as I paid attention to Kim paying wholehearted attention to me. "Of course. What do you need?"

"Promise me you will meet me here every day for lunch. I need some Antigone time to keep me sane from the drama in the drama studio." He had the confidence of a prince and the tenderness of a lost boy.

I returned his smile. "Of course. Same time tomorrow!"

Nineteen

FIDGE: How can you get detention in a holiday camp?

ME: I was late back from lunch with my friend

FIDGE: The Ts were late!?!

ME: Lunch with Kim, but it's fine
We had a good time

FIDGE: Nooooo
You're hanging out with the mean girl?

ME: I started the "Where's Waldo?" video. We're making some more now

FIDGE: Nice 👌

My routine for the week was set. A morning of pottery, which to my surprise I had suddenly really got into. The clay was spongy and soft, and just rolling it around in my hands gave me ideas. It smelled musty, like standing backstage among old lights and dusty costumes. And although it didn't do what I wanted it to, Miss Tanner was pretty good at showing me some hacks to get the idea from my brain into the clay in my hand. Amelie was right, the teachers were strict but spectacular. From class it was straight into lunch with Kim, which was beginning to feel more and more like a coming-of-age movie. He was open and kind, and never ran out of stories, some hilarious, some shocking. Another session of pottery and then the whole evening it was just me and the Ts working on our video. Talia and Tawny were both naturals in front of the camera and understood comedy like professionals. If I thought I had a good idea, they could make it one hundred times better . . . and stranger, which oddly was also better!

I felt as though I had found an awesome crew. Fidge was brilliant and Ismene was my sister-buddy – they were still my favourite people for sure – but I had never had my own girl gang before, and as much as I did *not* want to be called a "T", hanging out with Talia and Tawny was so much fun. And Teresa dialled in on a video call so often she felt like one of the team. We spent hours each night scouring locations, framing shots, editing clips together. I knew with confidence that Friday's video would be a huge success.

And deep down I hoped it would be enough to impress Kim; to convince him that Talia and Tawny were totally worth knowing and remembering, and that Antigone Kingsley was as awesome in real life as she appeared online.

Twenty

On Friday morning I ran to the drama studio fifteen minutes before the bell rang for lunch. Thanks to our now shared affinity with clay, Miss Tanner was more than happy to let me finish a little early and since I was desperate to find Kim before our new video went live, I ran through the halls at full speed.

By the time I reached the studio I was out of breath and feeling flushed. Kim stood by the door, spinning a diablo across a long piece of rope. I knocked on the window and motioned for him to come over.

"You're early," he said. "Are you crossing over to the dark side after all?"

Kim was grinning as I tugged on his sleeve to join me in the corridor. "Look, my new video is going live in fifteen minutes, but I wanted you to see it first!" I handed him the phone with the video primed and ready to go. My heart was pounding. I had forgotten how energizing it was to have your audience stood right in front of you.

Kim took the phone and leaned against the wall looking like a fashion model as he hit play. I looked on tentatively as Kim watched Tawny parade around in her red-and-white striped hat.

"Tig! There you are!"

I spun around to see Amelie. I ran my eyes across her face, quickly trying to decipher her mood. "Amelie! Hi! Where is Ismene?" As soon as I said my sister's name she appeared in the doorway with Amelie. "I've missed you guys. You've been so busy."

They both looked confused.

"We haven't been busy! We've been in the canteen every day, looking for you. Where have you been?" Ismene looked and sounded stressed. The kind of stressed she gets when she is worried about me.

I looked over at Kim and hoped he wouldn't notice, but he was busy on my phone. "Sorry. I came to find you on Tuesday, but you were rehearsing for your show, so—"

"What show?" Amelie's eyes had hardened into a cold stare as her words cut across me.

Why was she so mad? A familiar sense of dread swelled in the pit of my stomach.

"What show, Antigone? Where did you get that information from?"

"I saw you putting stage make-up on . . . and Kim said you were rehearsing—"

"Kim?" Amelie shouted.

I looked over to Kim, embarrassment blasting through my skin, but he smiled and winked at me.

He understood Amelie's little outbursts, and her fury seemed to roll over him like a passing cloud. He was still on my phone – that video seemed to be lasting for ever! I looked back towards Amelie. She was livid. She pulled me into the drama studio and marched me to the furthest corner of the room, with Ismene scurrying alongside her. My eyes darted around the room as my mind went to a thousand places. I saw Maddie and thought of her reckless dad. There was Louis with the partying uncle, Aurelia, who had sided with Amelie against Kim. There were lights, costumes, scripts, props and many other things I loved in this world.

"Antigone, are you listening to me?" Amelie was still ranting at me. She seemed so frustrated and I had no idea what I was supposed to have done wrong.

I looked at Ismene in the hope that she would provide me with some answers. Her face was deeply concerned as she reached out a hand to my arm. "Tig, Amelie is trying to help you. You have to stay away from Kim."

What? That was what all this hysteria was about? The cool guy who took me to lunch every day and paddled in the stream with me and shared stories about his whole world – *he* was the reason she was so mad?

My embarrassment took a sharp turn and I felt myself on a familiar road to rage. "Unbelievable! You two are unbelievable. First you dump me in a pottery camp with strangers, then you don't bother to message me or find me or even ask how I am getting on. And as soon as I find a good person—"

"Kim is not a good person, Tig! Look, ask Aurelia. She . . ."

I looked at the girl standing behind Amelie. She wasn't quite the confident, dazzling mean girl Kim had described her as, but still, he was my friend and if there is one thing I like to be, it's loyal, so I said, "Yeah, Kim told me about you and Aurelia, and I wasn't that surprised, especially not by you, Amelie."

Amelie spun back around to me, looking as though she was about to pull her own eyes out.

Ismene stepped in closer, turning my face gently towards her. I saw Aurelia slip away into the background. "Antigone, Amelie isn't trying to make things bad for you. We thought you had been with your pottery friends all week."

I let out a snigger, because . . . really? Pottery class? As far as they knew I still hated pottery.

Ismene kept speaking. "If we had known you were on your own, we would not have left you all week."

"I wasn't on my own. I was with Kim." I shrugged her hands off me.

Amelie came back to the conversation, but this time her tone was authoritative. "Tig, why did you come here today? Was it to see us, or Kim?"

I rolled my shoulders back, trying to throw off the weighty sense of dread pressing down on me. "I wanted to show Kim something on my phone." My phone! The mention of it made my stomach turn. Why *was* Kim still on my phone? "He still has it. I'd better go and get it." I turned to leave, but Amelie blocked me.

"Wait here."

She stormed out of the room and re-entered seconds later with my phone in her hand. She passed it straight to me. She seemed conflicted, a mash-up of anger, frustration and guilt all gleaming through her face. I wanted to ask her what was going on, but doing so would be to admit that I had no idea. It would mean admitting that I wasn't completely comfortable with how my week was going, or with Kim, or with pottery, or just being on the same freaking planet as everyone else.

"Antigone, you should not have been on your own all week." Amelie was furious, but it was unclear who her anger was directed at.

"Yes, I know. You can thank your mum for that."

Amelie's eyes were beginning to fill with tears, but her posture was energized and fierce. "You have to stay with us for lunch from now on and I am asking for you to be moved to our room."

That was the last thing I expected her to say. Four days ago I'd hoped she might fight to keep me in her and Ismene's little gang, but now things were different and I didn't really want to be stuck with the two of them bossing me around like a child.

"I don't *have* to do anything."

Ismene shuddered and I could feel her anxiety run through me like electricity. Did I mention already that my sister was deeply stressed?

Amelie said, "No, you don't, but we would really like you to stay with us now. I am sorry, Antigone. We should have been looking out for you." Her words were kind and restorative, but her fists were clenched, her jaw was tight, her breathing rapid and I struggled to read the situation.

"Yes, well, it's a bit late for that now."

I flounced past my sister and cousin like the victor at the end of a fight, only I had no idea what I was fighting for.

Twenty-one

My phone was going crazy in my pocket. I pulled it out and glanced down at the multiple notifications coming in through YouTube. This was not how Friday was supposed to go! My plan had been to show Kim the video first and then run back to the Ts just as it went live, so they could share in the moment and enjoy their success. Instead, I was storming through the corridors, unable to watch my video and feeling completely mad with my annoying cousin.

I grumbled out loud as the old Amelie popped up in my mind. You know – the one who stole my joy and overshadowed everything I tried to do. Yes, that one. I shook the thought out of my head. The most important thing now was to get back to Talia and Tawny.

I was almost at our dorm room when Jada came towards me – a big beautiful face glowing through the haze of chaos.

"Hey sweetie. I hear you're settling in well?"

I nodded at her. I didn't want to be rude, but I didn't want to miss my moment with Talia and Tawny either.

"Miss Tanner tells me you're working on an interesting piece – a tree or something?"

She wanted a chat and usually I would be up for it, but this time "Yes" was all she was getting.

There was a loud burst of laughter from a group of teenagers a little further away from us. They were huddled around a phone and I could hear the theme music from my YouTube channel playing. They were watching my video. This was insane. How many people here were following JustTigging? They must have just found me. Maybe it was the hashtags.

"Miss Tanner is an old friend of mine. We did Camp America together before coming here, so we know each other well."

But I hadn't used any hashtags.

"It's great that you are making new friends and trying new things. You must feel proud of yourself, sweetie."

More huddles of teenagers began to form, each staring down at a phone that was blaring out my theme music. Maybe Kim had added some hashtags? Maybe he'd shared it out or tagged people in it?

"I thought it might be good for us to catch up over the weekend? Perhaps you could show me your work in the art room?"

A whirl of laughter reverberated around the walls of Alpine. I scanned the groups huddled around phones. Everyone was laughing. This was incredible.

I was getting an "in the moment" reaction, and they LOVED it! My heart raced with a new kind of energy as anger was replaced with pure exhilaration.

One of the kids pointed to me, shouting, "Hey look, that's her, that's Tig! She is the one from JustTigging."

I could have leapt out of my own skin. I felt invincible. I looked down at my phone to see a blurred number of messages – too many for my brain to compute when there was so much going on.

"Antigone, what's happening? Have I missed something?" Jada was still speaking to me, the kids at Alpine were laughing and clapping, and then my phone rang with a call from Fidge, obviously calling to congratulate me.

I shoved my phone in my pocket and ran towards the dorm room as I called back to Jada, "Okay, thanks. Bye."

I needed to see Talia and Tawny. These girls had been a hit! I had made them a hit, and I couldn't wait to get back to our room and celebrate.

Twenty-two

"Have you seen it? What do you think?"

I burst through the dorm room door like a volcano on the verge of eruption, my heart racing as beads of sweat trickled down my back like molten energy. Talia and Tawny were huddled together on one of the beds and I bounded over to them before landing excitedly.

"Guys, the video! It's gone live! Have you seen it?"

Silence.

Tawny's cheeks were streaked with tears and her eyes were bright red. She had been crying. I registered her sadness, but not fully, because . . . I mean, had they *seen* the reaction to our video?

"*Everyone* is watching! It's huge. We did so well!"

More silence.

Tawny pulled her legs closer to her chest and dipped her head. She barely moved but I could tell she was crying. I shuffled closer and put my arm out to give her a hug, but to my horror Talia slapped my hand away.

"Ouch! Why did you do that?"

Talia turned to face me, her eyes blazing with fury. "Go away, Antigone!" Her voice was loud and confident, causing Tawny to flinch under its power.

I waited for more explanation, but when none was offered I pushed further. "Tawny, are you okay?"

"Of course she isn't okay, Antigone. How could you do this to us? We trusted you!"

My stomach swirled inside and my throat began to close as I looked at frail little Tawny crying in front of me. What had I done?

"I don't understand why you're upset."

"Oh really?" Talia pulled out her phone and thrust it towards me. "This is not what we agreed to make!"

I took the phone into my hands as though it was about to explode and pressed play on our YouTube video. Within three seconds it was clear it was not the video we made together. Someone had messed with the footage – they must have done. All of the clips of me introducing the game had been switched for clips of me in my old videos, and instead of Tawny playing along she looked like a freak, following me everywhere I went with arrows pointing at her saying "Spot the loser". There were screenshots of her mid-yawn, one with her eating a sandwich messily, another with her doing a weird dance. It was supposed to be funny, and it *was* funny when it was the three of us playing "Where's Waldo?", but now it looked awful and mean, and like the most embarrassing video I could possibly think of.

I searched my brain trying to understand how this could have happened. My hands shook and I wanted to convince Talia and Tawny that I absolutely did not make this video, but all of the words were hiding in the pit of my stomach and I couldn't make my voice work.

"Is everyone really watching it?" asked Tawny, her voice shaking as tears ran down her cheeks.

Even if I'd wanted to answer, Talia was leaving no space for me to speak: "How could you be so horrible? Why would you do this?"

"Please, I didn't mean to. I—"

"We know we are not the cool kids, Antigone. We are actually okay with that. Very many people think we are odd and we just ignore them. But you have made us look like . . ."

"I'm sorry. I didn't mean to. I don't understand . . ."

"How can you *not* understand? We can all see what you did!"

My phone began to ring in my pocket. It had been ringing for a while. I tried to ignore it, but it just kept ringing. I pulled it out. It was Fidge.

"And still you are on your phone! What are you checking? All of your likes? Any new subscribers, Antigone?"

I quickly cancelled his call. He would know that video was not from me; he would probably take it down. I looked back to Talia and Tawny and tried to think of a strong enough sentence to make them be quiet and listen. What came out was: "Just stop talking for one second so I can THINK." It had sounded so much softer in my head.

Talia grew another foot in height. "You have humiliated us in front of everyone. You pretended to be our friend—"

Ding, Ding, Ding, Ding, Ding . . . Messages were coming through on my phone at record speed. I glanced down at the screen and saw they were all from Fidge.

Why did you make that?
Can you take it down?
It's not funny, it's cruel

My hands were already shaking but now they looked as if they were about to drop off.

"We are trying to talk to you! Hello? All you care about is your stupid phone!" Talia was shouting. Tawny was still crying, my phone was dinging and dinging and dinging.

"JUST LEAVE ME ALONE!" I exploded at the top of my voice. "I never asked to be here, I never asked you to be in my video and I never wanted to be a stupid T. . . Will you all go away!"

Inside, my head was crumbling in on itself. Outside, I was a raging bull. Tawny and Talia were both silent.

Suddenly the door opened and Jada walked in, looking forlorn and horribly disappointed. She must have seen it already.

"Antigone!" Her voice was smooth and sad as she looked from me to Tawny and Talia.

Ding, Ding, Ding, Ding, Ding, Ding . . . My phone chimed loudly over the silence, like church bells summoning me to my own funeral.

"I think you should give me your phone, Antigone."

That was the last thing I wanted to do. I needed to speak to Fidge. I needed to take the videos down. I needed to know if I had been hacked.

Ding, Ding, Ding . . .

"Come on, Antigone. Pass me your phone."

"No, please, I can't do that. You need to wait."

Ding, Ding, Ding . . .

"Antigone!" Jada was firm, her eyes focused solely on me.

I unlocked the screen and tried to quickly solve all of the problems exploding from this small chunk of metal and glass, but the messages were coming in too fast, with huge applause from YouTube, endless stress from Fidge and now a call from Ismene. My fingers hovered in a paralysis of indecision.

"Antigone, pass me your phone."

I wanted to say something wise and wonderful, to explain that I had never made that video and it was all going to be okay. I wanted to take down the video and release an apology. I wanted to call Fidge and Ismene, and I wanted to do it all at the same time. But the crying and the dinging and the missed calls, the huge emotions and Jada's sad eyes – it all became too much.

I threw my phone on the floor as hard as I could and stormed out of the room.

Twenty-three

"I managed to take them down before Jada came to collect our phones." Issy spoke calmly.

My first time inside Amelie and Ismene's dorm room and I was crumpled on the floor, with crusty dry tears pinching my face. Ismene had worked quickly and taken down the video within thirty minutes of it going live. She sat close to me, rubbing my back like Mum would have done.

Amelie paced. "I can't believe Jada took *our* phones too. What did we do wrong?"

Ismene shook her head, subtly trying to silence our cousin, and I realized it probably wasn't for the first time.

"It is so embarrassing. I have been coming here for years and never once received even a stern word. Now I am stuck with the naughty kids and my phone has been confiscated."

I heard my sister tut, and while I appreciated her loyalty, I couldn't help but let out a sad little laugh. "Call it payback for you making me turn into a hysterical nutcase when you visited my school last summer. I was cool before you came along."

Amelie smiled back and for a moment we all sat with a slurry of memories.

"What did Jada say?" It pained me to say her name. I really liked Jada, and now . . . I winced as visions of myself throwing my phone across the room burst into my imagination.

"She was worried, but also pretty mad," said Ismene. "She said there was no way any of us would have phones for the rest of camp. But like I said, I deleted them both, so problem solved. Maybe a phone break is exactly what we all need."

Amelie groaned as my sister tried to sound positive.

I enjoyed three seconds of light relief before Ismene's words finally sunk in. "What do you mean, *both*?"

"The videos. I deleted them both. I assumed you didn't want to keep them?"

My heart started trembling again. I had seen one video – *one*! A horrible tribute to poor Tawny, who would never speak to me again. What was the other one?

"Issy, what is both? What does that mean? The video of Tawny . . . and what else?" I was barely making any sense as words were tripping up on their way out of my mouth.

Issy looked over to Amelie and I saw them both silently debate who should break the bad news to me.

"Talk to me! What is both?"

It was going to be Amelie. She sat down beside me and spoke in the softest voice I had ever heard her use. "There was a video about Fidge."

That was it. That was all she gave me. I sat bolt upright and held my breath, waiting for the rest of the story. Ismene took over. "It was about three minutes of him being crazy. It looked like videos you guys had made together just messing around, but edited into a montage that was, you know, a bit . . . And then there was this text written all over it . . ." Ismene stopped. It was bad, I knew it was bad.

"Come on, just tell me! What did it say?"

Amelie and Ismene looked at me awkwardly. They barely moved. It was as though I was a delicate but wild animal and the next few words would either break me or send me savage.

"Will one of you tell me? What did it say?"

Ismene took a deep breath and squinted her eyes as she spoke, anticipating a tornado of tears. "It said stuff like 'Biggest loser crushing on the cool kid', or something like that."

I gasped as my sister fell silent.

Amelie added, "It had hearts and lovestruck eyes all over Fidge, with you giving him the side-eye so it was really clear that you think he is an idiot and he just follows you around. It was so fake and immature. Nothing like your usual content."

She was trying to make me feel better, but it was pointless. The facts were too busy slapping me in the face. I tried to breathe out, but my lungs remained trapped in a gasp as the full extent of the damage unfolded before me.

"It's okay, Tig, I took them down. They were live for no more than thirty minutes." Ismene looked pale as she spoke.

I could barely utter: "But he was calling me and messaging me, and I declined them all. I didn't know." My voice was strained and even I couldn't tell if I was minutes away from exploding or minutes away from dissolving into a sloppy pile of mess on the carpet.

Ismene wrapped her arms around my shoulders. "I've dealt with it. It's all finished now."

"So, what did he say?"

There was a quiet pause as I waited for Ismene to continue soothing me.

"Ismene? What did he say?"

Still nothing. A horrible weight gathered in my feet and slowly took hold of my legs, my stomach, my chest, my throat.

"Ismene, when you spoke to Fidge, when you 'dealt

with it' before Jada took all of our phones – what did he say?"

I knew the answer then. I could tell by their frozen looks of horror that neither of them had spoken to Fidge. All of those unanswered calls. I imagined my phone sitting at the bottom of a filing cabinet in Jada's office, ringing and ringing, with Fidge on the other end. He must have felt so betrayed. As far as he knew I had made a humiliating video about him and plastered it on YouTube, ghosted all of his messages, cancelled his calls and now I had fallen off the planet altogether.

A low and painful groan rose from my belly. "No, no, no, no, no . . ." That was all I could say. Again and again, as Amelie and Ismene sat quietly beside me.

I had dealt with a fair few dramas over the years, but the agony of humiliating my best friend and not being able to fix it was the worst of them all. There are only so many times you can mess up before the hard truth finally sinks in. I was a disaster. I was a mess. I was a horrible, horrible person.

PART THREE

Twenty-four

Amelie and Ismene had become my crew. No, they had become my bodyguards. I may not have been allowed to switch dorm rooms, but that didn't stop them from spending every waking moment with me. They were at my door the second I woke up and escorted me back each evening in time for bed. We ate breakfast, lunch and dinner together, spent all our free time with each other and, aside from the classes, we were inseparable.

My first full weekend at camp included a trip to Geneva, where the three of us ate phenomenal amounts of chocolate, walked along the riverside and wandered through pebbled streets. We visited an old church, drank fresh water from city fountains and marvelled at how a place could be a bustling city, spotlessly clean and reasonably quiet all at the same time. In the evenings we played volleyball outside before watching comedies until our eyes were pleading for sleep. My mind was busy and my heart was happy. Most of the time.

Whenever there was a quiet moment, though, my thoughts would trail off into a deep dark forest in my mind, where all my buried problems lurked. I had three horrible paths to venture down. First and foremost, the one leading to Fidge. My oldest friend and biggest champion probably thought I made those videos and didn't care to explain why I did it. He might have thought I was completely ghosting him and couldn't care less about how he felt. He might never speak to me again. The moment I hit the reality of our broken friendship my heart would ache so much that I would jump off that path and start a new one. Tawny and Talia probably thought I hated them; that I'd made the videos to humiliate them. They probably thought I considered them pathetic and boring, the way everyone else did. Frustration would start to rise in my throat, and I would leave that trail of thought too, and move on to problem number three: Kim! Why had he not checked in on me? We had been hanging out every day, so why the sudden absence? My stomach would tighten as the image of him holding my phone was emblazoned across my eyes. He could have changed my films, but he wouldn't do that to me. Would he?

My brain was exhausted, leaping from one bad thought to the next. I was used to having my parents or Fidge, or even Taco, listen to me ruminate on all the miserable possibilities. Misery loves company, you know! I felt so trapped inside my own head I even drew a picture of JC doing the peace sign on a small piece of paper. The image had once been a print on a discarded prop under the Old Nic stage, but since moving the picture to my bedroom last summer, JC had become my no-judgement listening post. Even having JC drawn by me (and I am no artist, as we know) on a piece of folded paper in my back pocket could be just enough to pull me out of the forest of sadness in my mind.

It was the early hours of Monday morning when I finally broke. In the silence of our sleeping dorm room my brain flicked rapidly through a long list of unwelcome thoughts. Fidge must be really devastated with me. I sucked at pottery, my work looked ridiculous. Everyone at camp thought I was horrible. What did my friends in Brinstock think of the video? Had they seen it? Fidge must be so confused. Did my parents know I was in pottery class? Did I remember to empty the bin in my bedroom back home, because if not that must really stink now? Fidge – did he hate me?

My brain felt like a lonely swing in an empty garden, being battered around by a hurricane. Thoughts swept in and out at rapid speed, and no matter how hard I tried I couldn't drown out the noise in my head. Talia and Tawny had been asleep since I tiptoed into the room and as much as I wanted to wake them up and plead for them to hear me out, the idea of having a conversation felt too overwhelming.

I swung my feet out of bed and cooled my toes on the wooden floor. The night was silent and still. I scanned the room and saw two sleeping lumps snuggled under bed covers, two neatly stacked suitcases, and then mine, spilling with clothes. I didn't belong in the room, or camp, or as part of the three Ts.

I stood to my feet in frustration. I didn't care what they thought. When I went home, I never had to speak to these people again. It would all be over soon.

The thought comforted me for a sweet second before another hurtled towards me. But Fidge. FIDGE! I cared about *him*. What if he hated me for ever? What if my whole life slipped into a lonely void of nothingness because of some dumb video?

My heart began to pick up speed as a moment of clarity dawned on me. My Alpine adventure would vanish from my world soon, but Fidge was *home*. I could lose Alpine, but I couldn't lose Fidge.

Before I had the chance to talk myself out of it, I was walking through the sleeping halls of Alpine looking for one thing: Jada's office. I needed to get my phone back. I needed to call Fidge.

The floor was cold on my feet and there was barely enough light to see where I was going, let alone spot an intruder who wanted to kidnap me. (Is it just me or does everyone feel like they're about to get kidnapped in the middle of the night?) I had no concrete idea of where Jada's office was, or if she even had one, but there was a staffroom, and if I could get in there, then I might have a chance of finding her office, or the phone, or an incriminating clue about who sabotaged my videos and my life.

I crept stealthily through the heavy wooden staffroom door. Large windows ran along one wall, giving me just enough moonlight to adjust my vision. There were low comfy chairs, and coffee tables, a small kitchen with mugs drying on a draining board and shelves running across the walls. All completely empty. I sighed heavily, because of course they were empty! School was shut. What did I expect? That Alpine Adventure had a bustling office for two weeks where Jada kept all of the phones she confiscated, along with files labelled "Who ruined Antigone Kingsley's life"?

I threw myself into a chair and covered my eyes, feeling flat and defeated.

All of a sudden, a burst of light flooded the room and a harsh voice called out, "What are you doing?"

I screamed loudly and thrust my knees into my chest defensively, adrenaline rushing through my veins like an electric shock. My heartbeat was loud in my ears, and it took me a moment to process the now-lit room before the angry figure before me became a reality.

"Antigone? What are you doing?" Jada's face was set like stone as her hand rested against the light switch on the wall. In my head, I was explaining very eloquently why I was there, but in reality my voice was stunned to silence and my body trembled from head to toe with nervous energy.

"You scared me," was all that tumbled out of my mouth.

"So I see." Jada pushed herself away from the wall and walked towards me. I shuffled in my seat, my knees still protecting my chest as my fingers ran anxiously up and down my legs. As much as I knew Jada and trusted her warm hugs, my body couldn't seem to calm from the scare. I needed to laugh or cry to release some tension, but Jada wasn't in the mood for either.

"Why are you creeping around the staffroom at two in the morning, Antigone?"

"Why are *you*?" I blurted out. I didn't mean to sound rude, but my social brain was still asleep, it seemed.

A glimmer of a smile flashed in Jada's eyes. Then she reset her strict face. "That is rude, Antigone."

"Yep, sorry. I didn't actually mean that." I gasped in some more air as Jada continued to wait for an explanation. My voice was shaky as I spoke. "I would like my phone back, Jada."

There was silence.

"I thought it might be in here."

Jada was unmoving. Another thought popped into my head.

"Do you sleep in here?"

Jada let a little giggle slip out before replying firmly, "No, I am on night duty this evening, just for a few hours."

I nodded my head. The light had been on long enough for my fear to dissolve a little. I took a deep breath and closed my eyes. A thick bubble rose up in my throat and my chest tightened. My cheeks became wet with tears and my lips trembled as I swallowed hard the temptation to fall to pieces.

"Antigone, what is going on?" Jada's velvety voice reached inside me. I tried to answer with words, but only heavy sobs came out, tumbling into the room with brutal honesty. She sighed and sat beside me. My stomach wrenched as too many tears fell from too many thoughts. I craved my parents, Fidge, my sister . . . my freaking cat! I ached for something safe, someone who knew me, some place where I didn't have to keep pretending.

"Jada, are you going to give me my phone back?"

There was a momentary pause before she answered simply, "No."

Jada was tired, I could sense her exhaustion. She was sitting in a cold staffroom in the middle of the night with a girl she barely knew, who was sobbing because she wanted her phone back. From her point of view, I must have looked pathetic, like one of those kids who lives for their phone. I didn't want it for the social media or the games, or for whatever other reason grown-ups assume makes us all phone obsessed . . . I wanted it for my friend. I wanted it to fix things.

My brain was deflated and my voice had lost its power. I didn't know how to explain how wretched I felt or why those two videos on my YouTube channel had made it seem as though my whole universe had been shaken up and then thrown aside.

I tried again, just in case. "Are you sure?"

"Yes. Sorry, Antigone, but no phone until you go home."

I stood to my feet, defeated. "Okay, goodnight."

I left the room and went to bed. I barely slept.

Twenty-five

You can do this, Antigone. Just slap on that big bright smile of yours and be *the sunshine!*

I swooped into the art studio on Monday morning with a simple mission: to find a friend! Talia and Tawny hadn't arrived – I'd been careful to leave the dorm first – and the room was occupied by teenagers sitting quietly at individual desks. I made a quick analysis of each person, to see which one to target as friend-for-the-week material. There was one guy on his phone with music in his ears, another guy on his phone with cookies on the table, a girl not on her phone but listening to music and reading a book. Everyone in the room seemed locked into their own little bubble and I could see no way of penetrating their solitude.

Right . . . fine . . . I would talk to the whole room then!

I walked into the middle of the studio, took a deep breath and called out in my very best, bright and breezy stage voice, "Morning, everyone!"

It must have been unexpected, as I grabbed everyone's attention at the same time. I kept talking: "I hope you all had a good weekend?"

There was an awkward silence, but that was to be expected.

I continued: "I went into Geneva – for the first time actually – *such* a beautiful city!" I felt like a younger version of my mum, which was fine since everyone loves her. No one was answering me, but I was undeterred. "It was great to explore the local culture, you know? How about you guys? Anyone do anything nice?" I noticed a few people glance at each other, clearly wondering who this insane girl was and why she thought humans should talk to each other on a Monday morning. I shuffled on my feet and tried to keep my brave face on. "No? Well, next weekend we will all be going home. Crazy, huh?! Time flies, right?"

You see, *this* is why sometimes you have to talk to your reflection in the mirror or a pencil drawing of JC. It was a tough crowd. I searched my brain trying to find common ground for us all to gather on. I mean, it shouldn't have been that hard, since we were literally a team.

A *team*! The hike – that would grab their attention.

"I am *so* excited about our team hike in a few days. How about you guys?"

Again, strange looks were exchanged around the room.

"Put your hands up if you have done the hike before." I cringed inside as I tentatively demonstrated raising my hand in the air. What was I doing? I was no longer sounding like my mum and more like a classroom teacher. I kept my hand in the air, but no one joined me. The awkwardness levels in the room rose to astronomical as my cheeks flushed pink.

"You – John. Is that your name?" I picked on the kid nearest to me, who helpfully had a book on his desk with his name written on it.

John nodded. I think I was scaring him.

"Good! Well, John, are you looking forward to the hike?"

John's eyes skirted around the room looking for help from his peers before saying, "I never hike. None of us do. Just the girls who sit there." He pointed casually to *their* desk, Talia and Tawny's.

"Well, that's no good. Come on, guys. We're a team, right? Let's do this together, show those other guys what us brown tees are made of!"

There was a hush around the room.

"John, are you in?"

John looked at me like he wished I didn't know his name.

"Come on, John, let's hike together!"

His cheeks flushed pink – pinker than mine, I think

– as he said again: "No one hikes, except the girls who sit there." He grabbed hold of the book in front of him, opened it at a random page and pretended to read.

I looked around for another potential friend, but a ripple of activity scattered over the room as everyone suddenly became mysteriously busy. I stood for a few seconds more in the hope of finding a way to rescue my attempt at making friends. It was nearly nine o'clock and I knew Talia and Tawny would be in the room soon. I also knew that I was no longer welcome to sit at their table in art class, so I found a place to sit alone.

From that moment onwards I focused on the clay in front of me like it was my best friend, my only friend, because it kinda was! I didn't care who was in the room or out of the room. I had no interest in what everyone else was making. I just channelled every piece of my attention to the tree and owls that were forming out of the clay.

Whenever a thought came about Fidge, or Tawny and Talia, my heart would swirl around in my chest and a pulse ran through my body. If a memory of Kim flashed into my mind, a ball of rage ignited in my stomach. But there was nothing I could do and I couldn't be in constant turmoil, so I shook them from my mind, took deep breaths and continued to shape the clay.

Twenty-five

By Thursday lunchtime I almost had something I could be proud of. Almost. If I could only get those owls the way I wanted them! Miss Tanner had dismissed us early since it was officially the final class of the trip before our big hike. She and I stood, shoulder to shoulder, as we stared intensely at the clay I had spent the previous ten days with.

Miss Tanner broke the silence with an affirmation of my work. "This owl has a curious look."

"It has wonky eyes."

"It has excited eyes."

We continued to stare at the three little birds.

I said, "The feathers are messy."

"The feathers have movement."

"It is short and squatty."

"It is small and cosy."

"I hate it," I groaned, then grabbed the clay.

I was about to squash it into a pancake on the table when Miss Tanner placed a gentle finger on my hand. "You're going to give up on it already?"

Already!? I had spent the last two weeks working on that project. Before Switzerland my longest art project had been a three-hour papier-mâché snowman at Christmas.

"It's not perfect," I said. "Owls don't look like *that.*" I gestured miserably towards the birds.

"Antigone, I am sure there is some magical app that can 3D print a perfect replica of three owls to go into your tree. You can probably download it for a few dollars. Turns out perfection is pretty cheap these days."

I understood her tone. It was just the kind of thing my parents would say. "I don't mean they have to be perfectly the same, but I do want people to look at it and know what they are."

"So, it'll be perfect when enough people say that it is?"

"I guess."

"Then you are confusing perfect with popular."

I couldn't help but groan. It was hard enough trying to grasp art. Now she wanted me to do some philosophy too! "I don't understand what you want me to do," I said. "Am I supposed to put three rubbish birds on the tree and not care, or work on them for another week and not give up?"

Miss Tanner looked pensively at my tree before picking up the smallest owl and placing it gently in her palm. "Have you heard of the famous Italian sculptor Michelangelo?"

"Of course. My parents love all the ancient stuff."

Miss Tanner giggled, showing me a glimmer of fun beneath her cool exterior. She placed my owl back in the tree and then stood up with a fresh piece of clay, rolling it around her hand as she spoke. "Well, Michelangelo was an incredible sculptor actually. One day he was asked how he managed to create such a magnificent sculpture of King David. He answered, 'I saw the angel in the marble and carved until I set him free.'"

She paused and looked at me for a brief second before resuming her clay rolling. "You see, Michelangelo believed that the art of sculpting was not about imposing a standard, or a popular idea or look, onto a block of marble, but rather about finding the beauty that already existed within the stone."

Miss Tanner was gazing intently out of the window, a strip of light running down her face as though she was half in the room and half outside. Outside searching for beauty, probably. A moment more of silence and she turned on her heels, joining me at the art table. "In other words, Antigone, stop looking for everyone else's idea of perfect and look at what's in front of you. The more you look for the hidden beauty in a boring lump of clay, the more it will appear."

I stared again at the birds. Hidden beauty in a boring lump of clay?

I became so preoccupied by my squatty little bird that I hardly noticed when Jada entered the room.

"Hey Antigone! Are you doing some overtime on your project?"

My cheeks flushed red, but I could see from her relaxed posture that she wasn't clinging on to any anger from our last encounter. I smiled at her and looked back over to the birds. I knew Jada and Miss Tanner were friends and assumed they had things to chat about and lunch to eat. I could hear the two of them whispering in the background, but I paid no attention. My mind was busy on a loop, searching for beauty in a boring lump of clay. Was it small and cute, or short and squatty? Were those eyes wonky or energized? Did they look inconsistent or different?

I scoured every lump and bump of the clay for as long as I could, but found no hidden beauty. Maybe it was there but I couldn't see it. Although, the more I stared at those three little birds, the more I liked them. They were odd and quirky – I mean, how could wonky be boring anyway? And those feathers were completely scruffy, but I loved scruffy! Scruffy was unpredictable and fun. And that curious look Miss Tanner mentioned – it was intriguing and a little bit adorable. It was odd: the clay wasn't changing – I had not made any tweaks or adjustments – but I was changing my mind. I was well on my way to really liking those owls!

"So this is the famous tree and owls you have been working on." Jada stood next to me, the scent of her rich perfume taking me back to the early days of Alpine Adventure.

"Yes, I am nearly finished."

Jada studied them carefully, searching my work for meaning, thinking out loud: "So the tree represents life . . . or home . . . No, Switzerland! The tree represents Alpine Adventure in Switzerland."

I smiled as Jada kept on looking.

"And the three owls are all the nature outside . . . No, the owls are your dreams!"

Miss Tanner laughed as she came to join us. "Come on, Jada, you gotta do better than that."

The three of us looked again at the little clay sculpture soaked in sunshine.

"Okay. I got it, Antigone. The three owls represent you, Amelie and Ismene, right?" Jada looked delighted with herself, as though she had figured out the answer to a million-dollar question.

I smiled and shrugged my shoulders before looking again. Was it me, Amelie and Issy? It didn't feel like it.

"Come on, sweetie. Am I right?"

I looked over to Miss Tanner, who was smiling at her friend, hoping she would tell me what the three birds were supposed to be.

"Don't look at me for answers, Tiggy Tig Tig. You made it!"

Twenty-six

Alpine Adventure was abuzz with activity. The zeal of victory-hungry teenagers hung in the air like static electricity. It was hike day, finally! The moment everyone had been waiting for. The only reason some people even came to Alpine.

Base camp was awash with teenagers as teams readied their hiking boots and meticulously devised their plans through crumpled maps. I scoured the groups, not really sure what I was looking for. I wanted to find some yellow tees, but they were not my team. I could look for the brown, but they weren't going to be looking for me, let's face it. The more I searched for someone familiar, the more I realized just how small I was. To me Alpine was Tawny, Talia, Kim, Amelie, Ismene, Jada and Miss Tanner. In reality, Alpine was hundreds of teenagers in tees of virtually every colour of the rainbow and I had never even noticed them before.

I found a group wearing lilac. Lilac! Why couldn't I have been dumped in lilac? It was so much prettier than brown. I tried to guess their activity from afar. They were like the pages of an outdoor-fashion magazine. Their backpacks weren't just backpacks; they were sleek, high-end designer packs in shades of alpine white and glacier blue. They had more pockets than anyone could possibly need, each filled with neatly folded gear. This wasn't a race; this was luxury hiking at its finest! My guess was they were studying fashion, or economics, or just general poshness. I glanced over to another group in royal blue, who were distributing food wrapped in beeswax between each other's backpacks. Matching bags, matching food covers, matching hats – at a guess I would say culinary. Or perhaps sewing class? It was kind of hard to guess when you went to a school that was basically maths, English, science, history, geography. . .

My thoughts were hijacked by chanting: "We're the Mountain Maulers, no mountain is too tall! If you can't hike with Maulers, you can't hike at all!" A gang of strikingly strong teenagers weaved through the crowds like an American soccer team ready for the playoff. A puff of excitement reached me as they wafted past, their huge arms making their rucksacks look small and inadequate. What was this world I was living in? I couldn't imagine anyone from Brinstock singing about being a "Mountain Mauler" or carrying matching designer rucksacks. No one at my school would even care about hike day. The nearest thing we have is sports day at the end of the year and most people take it as an opportunity to lay on the grass and chill. It's only the sporty kids who get involved – which is about ten kids in total!

I giggled and looked around for someone to share it with. Buried between kids in various coloured tees and backpacks and huge maps I saw a flash of a yellow tee, and without checking to see who it was I charged straight towards them. I was so concerned the person would slip away that the moment I was in grabbing distance I tapped on their shoulder, squeezing my arms through a group of vivacious teenagers in lime green.

Instantly the person spun around. "Hey, Tiggy Tig Tig. It's been a while."

My heart sank a million times over as Kim moved through the group of teenagers and stood right in front of me. His eyes were sparkling and his smile was broad and white. He looked exhilarated, like someone who already held the victory. My stomach was flipping over as I tried to figure out if his obvious joy was the thrill of the hike, or the thrill of sabotaging all my friendships through two cruel videos. It had to be the hike, right? He couldn't be that dark.

"How has your week been?" Kim was completely calm.

I scrambled to find an appropriate response. "It was good."

"Nice." Kim was still smiling.

Everything in me wanted to shout, *What happened to you? Why didn't we meet up every day like last week? Why didn't you care that I had a huge trauma with my YouTube and my best friends? Was it* you*? Did you make those videos?*

Kim was so placid, it felt presumptuous to say anything at all. I mean, we had only met a few times; it wasn't like he had to meet me for lunch or care about my friends. We had known each other for less than a week. I felt foolish for thinking he would even be bothered.

Kim was not rushing to speak, so I quickly filled the silence. "I love your rucksack. You look very prepared." That was the dumbest line. I didn't love his rucksack and he knew I didn't.

Kim smiled some more, still not speaking.

"So, the big day is here. I know you love a hike. Who is in your team?"

"Just some of the guys from drama who I usually hike with. You are stuck with the Ts in brown again – sounds thrilling." He sniggered and a glimpse of his mean side shone through his charm. His eyes were glowing with excitement as his silky black hair swept across his face. I didn't know whether to hate him or beg him for one more lunch. What I did know was that I felt stupid. Silenced. As though the moment I saw him all my power fizzled out like a bath bomb and I was a gloopy mess standing on a pile of mud.

I considered walking away, or shouting, or making friends again. I wanted to do *something.* What was I waiting for? Permission?

Kim knew he had me in complete confusion and didn't seem to care. "See you around, Tiggy Tig Tig."

He turned to walk away, and I was about to let him, but an image of Fidge, Tawny and Talia was projected so strongly on my mind it was like they were there with me. I knew I owed it to them to find out the truth.

"Did you make the videos?" My voice shook as I spoke.

Kim moved back towards me. "You're still going on about that? Why did you take them down?" Kim was slow – he spoke slowly, smiled slowly, blinked slowly.

I was running out of oxygen as it became harder and harder to breathe. "Why did you do that? Why did you upload them? I thought we were friends."

"Did you?" He shrugged.

Did I? Why did I think that? It was only a few. . . I shook the thoughts away from my mind. "Yes, I did. You said I made camp 'bearable' for you, remember?"

"Oh, did I? No, Antigone, sorry. I don't remember." He laughed again but never once removed his gaze from me.

My voice was barely working, my breathing was rapid and I should have walked away, but I was getting angry, which meant I couldn't back down.

"We had a date and you said—"

"A date? Is that what you thought it was?"

I was raging, trembling, embarrassed, powerless and determined all at the same time. "Whatever. You made the videos. I know you did. I trusted you with my channel and my thoughts and my phone. Just admit it – you did it!"

"Calm down, Tiggy. No need to lose it."

"Admit it. I know it was you."

"Wow, you get really crazy. I thought there was something odd about you."

There was silence. I was like a trapped mouse. If I lost it with him, I would prove him right about calling me "crazy". If I left and walked away, he might carry on being charming again, or he may be indifferent or unkind. He was confusing and terrifying, and I didn't want to be around him any more.

I turned on my heels. This time I would walk away.

The hum of excitable teenagers had cooled and now everyone was standing in their groups. I glanced across to Amelie and Ismene, ready in their yellow tees. They had been watching me speak to Kim. Then I saw Talia and Tawny, team brown waiting for their third team member. I started walking over to them, not sure what I would say once I got there.

Suddenly, Kim called out across the crowds, loud enough for everyone to hear, "Hey Tig, good luck with the hike!"

I smiled at him, because I was raised to be polite and that is what you do when someone says something friendly. But I wish I hadn't, I really wish I hadn't, because then he called out again, saying, "Don't worry about the videos; it was just a joke. You kept saying the Ts were weirdos, so I thought you would find it funny. Anyway, see you after the hike!" Then he turned and walked away.

I didn't need to turn around to see Talia and Tawny's faces. Their sadness was already etched into my mind. I knew everyone was looking at me. I knew everyone had heard.

Twenty-seven

"Okay, hikersssssss! Welcome to the annual Mountain Hike Extravaganzaaaaaaaa."

Hysteria rose from the crowd like a rainbow bubble, floating above our heads before bursting and sprinkling us all in fairy dust. The atmosphere was euphoric, electric, almost magical.

"Are you readyyyyyyy?"

"Yes, we are!"

"I said . . . are you readyyyyy?!"

"YES, WE ARE!"

Everyone hung on to the call-and-response like dogs waiting to be released off their leashes before bounding into a field of long grass. I looked around for the voice behind the microphone but all I could see were hundreds of eager faces. I stood next to Tawny and Talia, but I didn't dare look at either of them.

"Teams, this is your moment to prove your worth on the mountain. You have six hours to complete the course, using just your maps, your minds and what else?"

"TEAM WORK!" Voices resounded across the mountain.

"What else?"

"TEAM WORK!"

"Say it again . . ."

"Team work, team work, team work . . ." The reply tumbled into a chant as teams threw their arms around each other and slapped each other's backs in camaraderie.

When I'd first heard about the Friday hike, the sheer passion of the different teams and the famous trophy with the winning names engraved each year, the competitor in me craved the victory, but the teenager craved the freedom. Six whole hours in the big outdoors with no adults watching over us. It was going to be the highlight of my week. I desperately wanted to enjoy the chanting and get involved, but deep down the thought of hiking with Talia and Tawny and having no adult supervision was beginning to make me feel very uncomfortable. I mean, just how much *did* they hate me? Enough to ignore me, to steal my lunch, to lose me off a mountain?

I decided to take a quick glance over at them to try to suss out their game plan.

"Team work, team work, team work!" In true Tawny and Talia style the two of them were jumping up and down, squealing with unabashed joy.

My heart felt a pang of pain and pride. I was proud

that they could be humiliated and called weirdos in front of everyone yet still enjoy the moment completely as themselves, but it pained me that they believed I was the one wanting to humiliate them. What if I threw my arms around the two of them and joined in the chant? Maybe they would forgive and forget right there and then, and this whole thing would be swept away and forgotten about.

Talia saw me staring at her and Tawny. She protectively put an arm around Tawny before manoeuvring her away from me.

I guess not!

"Okayyyyy, hikersssss, gather in your groups. The race will start in five minutes."

I took a deep breath. There were hundreds of people standing at base camp but there were only two that I needed to spend the next six hours with. I had managed seven days of sleeping in the same dorm room only by leaving Amelie and Ismene once I knew the Ts were in bed, then pretending to be asleep as they tiptoed around the room getting ready for class in the morning. Pottery had gone by seamlessly as Miss Tanner was not one for idle chatter and I was so absorbed by my work I didn't really notice anyone else in the room anyway. But this time, communication was going to be unavoidable. In just five minutes' time

I would be hiking through a lonely mountain with literally no one else to talk to and nowhere else to go. It was me and them, and I needed to find a way to make it work.

I looked over to my ex-friends. Talia had two long plaits running down her back and a giant rucksack that was clearly meant for someone much bigger who would be hiking for much longer. The bag was stuffed to overflowing and she still had another hip bag wrapped around her waist, a water bottle hanging around her neck and snacks in both hands. Tawny had come ready for disaster, with thick sun block pasted onto her face like warpaint and a sweat band firmly set like a damn, desperately trying to hold back her thick orange hair from pouring into her face. She held a crumpled map in one hand and a bug swatter in the other. They were the least in-sync of all the teams, with no matching clothes or hats or bags. They didn't look like hikers, or even the kind of people that could read a map. They looked quirky, funny, a little bit odd. They looked the same way I always felt inside.

A strange thought flickered into my mind: What if these were my people? What if these girls were supposed to be my best friends for ever and I'd thrown it all away for lunch with K-pop Kim?

My stomach turned over as I measured the loss of Tawny and Talia and, worst of all, Fidge. I swallowed hard and took a deep breath. Everywhere around me people were bonding and preparing for the big race. I needed to get my head in the right space. I needed to be a part of my team.

"Okay, hikersssssss! To the starting lines." The crowd swelled with energy.

Without thinking I ran towards the Ts and blurted out, "We are in this together, right? I am in your team?"

Talia and Tawny nodded at me. As much as I wanted a "You sure are, Tiggy Tig Tig!" I was grateful for the nod.

"I have no idea where we are going. I haven't done this before. What do I do?"

Talia and Tawny looked at me thoughtfully. I don't think they were judging me – more trying to calculate who it was they were dealing with. Mean, sly YouTuber who faked friendship for popularity online? Or awkward English girl lost on a mountain, drowning under the weight of other people's expectations?

Twenty-eight

The second the gun fired, hundreds of teenagers ran in every direction. The perfect, the sleek, the victory-hungry – we all reverted to our five-year-old selves as we sprawled out over the mountain. Every team had a game plan and no two teams' plan looked the same. The Mountain Maulers fell silent as they disappeared over the pinnacle at lightning speed. The yellow tees jumped and leapt, and I swear I heard the first few lines of a musical being sung before they too vanished from view. The lilacs turned and ran in the opposite direction, away from the starting line. Clearly they were either geniuses or insane, but they were laughing loudly either way.

Tawny and Talia ran down the mountain, giggling as they tumbled over their own feet. I followed them as closely as I could, allowing my lungs to absorb the rush of cool mountain air as my legs leapt over the muddy mounds and long grass. All the stress and anxiety that had been swirling around my body seemed to be shaken away as adrenaline turned me from a lonely teenager to a mountaineering champion. I felt powerful, strong, alive . . .

Twenty-eight

I ran so fast my brain could no longer keep up with my feet. I ran until I overtook Talia and Tawny. I ran until my toes tingled inside my heavy walking boots. A narrow stream of water appeared ahead of me. I registered its width, guessed its depth, noted the rocks that could become obstacles, but I never stopped running. As the stream neared, I launched myself across it without hesitation and landed perfectly on the opposite side like a ninja. I kept running as fast as I could, not thinking about the race or the direction or the victory, just running. Every step made me feel more energized and free.

I looked around. There were no other teams nearby – we had outrun them all! The small win echoed around my body, and my legs responded by running even faster. There was a thick, dense forest ahead. There would be fallen logs, an uneven surface, I would have to dodge things at every level. I knew it would be tough to run through, but *I* was tough! I was ready! I entered the woodlands with the same speed and determination that had carried me down the mountain. A branch brushed across my face but I kept going. I ran directly into a spider's web and felt its sticky, stringy remains tack onto my cheeks, but that couldn't stop me either. I leapt over logs, trampled in animal poo and ducked under low-hanging branches. I could feel my blood hitting every part of my body.

There was a clearing further ahead in the woods. I had done it! I had battled through the rough terrain without hesitation and whatever was on the other side of that forest I would take that on too. I was invincible.

I pushed my way through the clearing and then stopped suddenly, my feet tentatively placed on the edge of a long winding road. My heart was pounding as my body tried to process the rapid need for extra oxygen. I looked around, trying to understand my environment. There was silence. No cars. No other hikers. Just a sign reading "Welcome to Alpine Adventure Youth Camp".

You have got to be kidding me.

The pieces of the puzzle jolted together. I had run down the mountain, away from base camp, and was standing just a two-minute stroll from the art block. My ears could feel the drum of my heart as beads of sweat rolled into my hair. I was soon to be less ninja and more lost, frizzy loser on the wrong side of the mountain. I growled out in frustration. It hadn't even occurred to me to check a map or consider where we were supposed to be going.

"Antigone?" Talia and Tawny emerged through the thickets, Talia panting from exhaustion and Tawny trying to remove twigs that had collected in her hair when she was racing to keep up with me.

Talia looked completely confused as she tried to gather enough breath to speak, while frantically waving a crumpled map in front of me. "Antigone, where are you going?"

Twenty-nine

It took an hour to walk back to the spot on the mountain where I'd overtaken Talia and Tawny – the spot where we were supposed to take a slight left, not head full speed towards the road.

Talia complained the whole way. "I have done this hike very many times and I know this mountain very well. I also have a map. A *map*. There is the real clue that you should be listening to me. Now I can't believe we have to do all of this walking again . . . Oh look, what a pretty tree, it seems familiar . . . Yes, that is it, because I saw it one hour ago when I nearly smacked my head into the branches trying to keep up with *Antigone*!"

On and on she moaned, this tiny Spanish girl berating me for not following *her* plan. Sure, I felt foolish and apologetic to begin with – for, like, the first ten minutes. But after that it was overkill. She needed to let it go. I mean, did she really need to keep making those ridiculous digs about me not *listening* or not *paying attention* or not *caring* enough? If there is one thing that really annoys me, it is when people tell me I don't listen or pay attention or care enough, because I do, I really really do. Every little bit of me works overtime trying to do whatever it is people expect of me and I don't know why it goes wrong, but sometimes it just does.

Hours passed and we had no sighting of any other team. Around lunchtime Tawny felt hungry but Talia insisted we march on through our lunch break, reminding her she could "thank Antigone" for that. After a while I managed to zone out her incessant talking and instead just plod obediently behind her, trusting it would be over soon enough.

It was in this act of blind walking, doing whatever Talia said and drowning out her moaning with my thoughts that I noticed something. Talia wasn't looking at the map either. Occasionally she would glance at it but not in any detail, not for long enough that she would actually know where we were going. Mostly she waved it around dramatically, using it to accentuate her frustration whenever she said, "You can thank Antigone for that too!"

I started watching Talia and Tawny closely, checking to see if either of them had a notion of which direction we should be heading in. Tawny was quiet, and while her powers of observation seemed to notice every rock, tree and blade of grass, it was obvious that she had no interest in where we were going. I am not sure she even remembered that we were in a race. And there was no way Talia could know. Partly because she never looked at the map, partly because she never stopped talking (and no one can talk for that long and still know where they are going), but mostly because it was late and we were still in the middle of nowhere. And because the small bridge we were about to walk across had the same mud-slide mark as the last bridge, when Tawny had slipped over onto her bottom. Meaning this bridge *was* the last bridge and we were completely lost!

"Right, that's enough, Talia. Give me that map." It was the first time I had spoken in hours and I underestimated the frustration in my voice.

Talia stopped and looked at me, outraged. "*You* want to see the map? Have you not been listening to me?"

"I think the whole mountain has been listening to you, Talia. Just give me the map."

"Antigone, I have been on this mountain very ma—"

"Very many times, yes I know. You mentioned it about five hundred times already. In fact the last time you mentioned it was when we were walking over this bridge three hours ago."

Talia looked around. Her eyes widened as she registered the slide mark where Tawny had slipped.

Still, she was not ready to lose the argument. "Don't be ridiculous, Antigone. That was over there." She flung her arms out, gesturing to the whole mountain.

"Yes, I think you may be right, Tiggy. Look, we are right by the Sorbus aucuparia tree with the small berries around the bottom. I was trying to pick some when I slipped. And look, my slip mark!" Tawny pointed to the bridge.

"There are very many trees and very many bridges; it's just a coincidence, Tony!"

Tawny nodded as Talia dismissed her.

"Don't agree with her, Tawny. You are right! We *have* been here before."

"You don't tell Tony what to do, Antigone."

"Why? Because that's your job? Stop bossing her around."

"I do not boss her around. I help her."

"Help her with what? She isn't a baby! You don't act like her friend. You act like her mother!"

"Oh, and you are a real friend, aren't you!"

Talia and I were arguing back and forth, each of us letting out all the frustration of the last few days.

"You think you are so perfect, don't you, Talia!"

"Do I, Antigone? Don't tell me – is that the title of your next YouTube video?"

In among all the chaos, Tawny tried to pacify us

both: "Come on, guys. We don't need to fight – let's keep going."

But neither I nor Talia was ready to stop.

"How many times do I have to say sorry for a video I didn't even make?"

"We watched you make it all week."

"Not that video, you didn't."

Tawny continued trying to calm us: "It doesn't matter. Let's just get back – it will be dark soon."

She began crossing the bridge, but I was so fixed on Talia that I misjudged the space between myself and Tawny. "Talia, when will you ever let this go?" I said as I flung my arm out dramatically, accidentally catching the bottom of Tawny's backpack. The momentum was so fast that before I could stop myself I had caused Tawny to lose her balance, and she slipped on the bridge, fell underneath the wooden rail and landed in the shallow, rocky stream underneath.

"Tonnnnyyyy!" Talia yelled as she ran to help. She covered Tawny in fuss and friendship, wrapping her arms around her and pulling her out of the water. Tawny was sitting up, perfectly still, with a few tears rolling down her cheeks. She was like a delicate little bird with a broken wing.

Ugh, why did people always get hurt when I was around?

Thirty

"Do you think you can stand up?" said Talia, seeming not to notice her feet getting wet by the stream. All her attention was on Tawny.

"I can try," Tawny snuffled, trying so hard to be brave.

"Okay, on the count of three . . . ready?"

Tawny nodded through tiny tears as she gripped on to Talia.

"One, two, three . . ." Both friends strained as hard as they could before collapsing back onto the ground.

I joined them tentatively, fully aware that since meeting them I had caused nothing but pain. "Can I help?"

Talia scowled at me, but knowing she had no choice moved aside so I could take one of Tawny's arms.

"Okay, let's go," I called out and instantly we managed to bring Tawny to her feet. She yelped in pain. "Talia, let's put her down by the tree. It's okay, we've got you."

We shuffled as best we could to the tree and made Tawny comfortable on the ground. I took off my coat and wrapped it around her shivering shoulders.

"Thanks, Tiggy."

Talia snuggled into Tawny to help keep her warm, but in all the commotion she had become just as wet as her friend. I grabbed Talia's backpack and started rummaging through it.

"Antigone, what are you doing?"

"I am looking for a blanket to warm you both up. You seem to have packed enough for an arctic expedition, so I am guessing you have a blanket, right?"

"You can't go through my bag without ask—"

"*Stop!*"

Talia fell silent at the sound of Tawny's thin voice, straining to shout.

"Both of you, stop arguing." Tawny was still weeping, still curled up like a wounded bird, but she was determined and strong. "This is crazy. We can't all hate each other for the rest of our lives. Understood?"

Talia and I nodded quietly, neither of us wanting to cause Tawny any more pain.

Tawny took a deep breath and continued talking. "Let me guess, Tiggy. You fell for the charms of Kim and in return he sabotaged your videos, right?"

A lump of sadness gathered in my throat as I nodded my head.

Tawny looked at me, her eyes filled with sincerity and compassion, before turning to Talia. "Talia, you are angry with Tiggy because you trusted her and she made us feel stupid, right?"

Talia frowned and nodded intensely at her friend.

Tawny smiled, her kind glance an invisible hug around Talia's shoulders. "Right, well, you can both be quiet now, because I have something to say."

Talia and I leaned in closer to listen.

"I have a lot of fun with you, Tiggy Tig Tig, and I want us to be friends."

"I want to be friends too!"

"I said I'm talking . . ." Tawny was firm, but in the dim light I could see a glimmer of a smile stretching on her face. "If you want to be a T, it comes at a price."

I nodded emphatically, like I was making a promise to a frail old lady on her death bed. "Anything, I will do anything!" I looked over at Talia, expecting to see her scowl, but her eyes were filled with tears as she listened to Tawny speak. As the evening drew in and the air became chilly, I was ready to pledge whatever price they wanted me to pay.

"Why did you show the videos to Kim?" Tawny asked.

I shuffled awkwardly on the floor. The cold, damp ground was beginning to soak through my trousers. "I don't know. Because I thought he was my friend, and I trusted him, I guess."

Tawny tried again. "Tiggy, you *ran* to show Kim the video. You were talking about him all week, about how excited you were for him to see it."

As she spoke, I could hear myself talking about him. I even saw myself typing about him to Fidge. I took a long, hard breath. I knew exactly why I needed him to see the video first. "I wanted him to like it. I wanted him to like you and think you were fun and exciting. I wanted him to like me." I could feel my cheeks glowing red and felt a flicker of gratitude for the growing darkness.

"And that is the rule about being a T, Antigone: you have to be yourself, whether anyone else likes it or not." Tawny reached out and squeezed my hand, turning that lump in my throat into blubbering tears.

"But Kim thought he knew me because of my channel, and I wanted him to be impressed by the real me."

"Kim is only impressed by Kim. You need to know this!" Talia still spoke with ferocity, but this time it felt like she was aiming her arrows to defend me rather than directly at me.

I laughed through messy tears. "Maybe."

"Definitely!" Talia grabbed hold of my other hand, making a little circle. It was a bit weird. I mean, my friends back in Brinstock would never . . . Ugh, whatever. We held hands, which was just what I needed! The night was creeping closer and closer as the hope of reaching the finish line drifted further and further away. We sat still for a moment, none of us thinking about how we might ever get home.

"It's really hard," I said, "because I want to be a T, but I hate disappointing people, and being me usually means I will definitely disappoint people. I mean, you have no idea about the chaos I caused last summer." Tawny and Talia were silent and for a moment I thought I was going to have to divulge the whole attempted murder thing all over again. I waited, praying one of them would speak so I didn't have to.

Talia squeezed my hand tighter. "You are a little strange, Tiggy Tig Tig, and Tawny does seem to have more accidents when you are around, but many people think you are great just the way you are – very many people, I am sure."

We all giggled hard enough to burst the tension and dissipate our tears. It's funny how being stranded on a mountain in the middle of nowhere can be just what you need to end an argument.

Thirty-one

We waited for hours, assuming that someone would come and rescue us. In my mind a group of Mountain Maulers were going to spring from behind some trees and carry the three of us back to base camp, where everyone would be waiting for us with warm blankets and mugs of hot chocolate. But once the sky was completely dark and our wet trousers had turned to ice, it became abundantly clear that the rescue mission was down to us.

I struggled to my feet. My bones ached, my body was frozen, my lips felt dry and parched. "Okay, Ts, since no one is coming to save us, I suggest we save ourselves."

Tawny and Talia looked up at me in helpless desperation. Tawny whimpered, "I don't think we can; it's too dark to see the map."

"Tawny is right – we will get lost."

"Well, I hate to break it to you, but we are already lost."

They huddled into each other like terrified kittens.

"Look, Tawny, you notice everything. I am sure if we pay attention and go slowly you will figure out the way back. And Talia, you can . . . I don't know . . . you can talk – talk us back?"

Tawny giggled. "We cannot sit here and wait; it's getting cold and creepy and we need to get home."

Talia stood up and between the two of us we pulled Tawny to her feet. She winced under the pressure, saying, "I don't think I can walk on it." Her voice was wobbly and I knew she was trying hard to hold everything together.

I tried to think quickly. "Okay, Talia, you carry my bag. Tawny, you carry your bag. And I will carry Tawny!" They both gawped at me, and I waited in hope that they might have a better idea . . . They had nothing. "Okay, Talia, take my bag?"

Talia obediently strapped my backpack across her chest like a baby chimpanzee clinging to its mother. I stood in front of Tawny and, with a strength I never knew I had, shimmied her onto my back. It was a good thing she was tiny!

"Now, Talia and I are going to be quiet while you, Tawny, lead the way."

It was the slowest, most painstaking hike known to humankind, but Tawny directed us, pointing out each twig, thorn, mud mound and brier on the way. My head hung low under her weight, and I could see no further than my own feet. But we kept going, kept trusting, kept hoping that we would find our way home.

Thirty-two

The whole way back to base camp – *the whole way* – I expected to see torches from a concerned search team desperately looking for the three missing teenagers, or hear the faint sound of worried strangers calling out our names. Instead we arrived back to a party! Not a search party or even a welcome party, no – a victors' party, filled with jubilant teenagers celebrating the end of their hike. The base of the mountain was lit up with lanterns strung across poles that hung over long trestle tables covered in food and drink. There was a barbecue, a campfire with people toasting marshmallows. There was music, there were people dancing – some guy was even juggling with fire. No one, not one single person, seemed to notice we hadn't come back.

I slid Tawny off my back, and my hands and legs shook with relief. The three of us stood under the glow of the lanterns, covered in mud, shivering cold and looking like the biggest losers of the hike.

"We made it!" Tawny said, trying to be positive.

"Looks like they really missed us," Talia laughed as she threw my backpack onto the floor.

In the distance I spotted a glimpse of yellow, and a surge of impatience to see my sister overtook me. "Look, I think it's Ismene. Come on, let's go."

Tawny wrapped her arms around my and Talia's necks and the three of us hobbled towards the yellow tees.

The moment she saw me, Ismene squealed in delight. "You're back. I thought we were going to have to send out a search party," she joked.

"Why didn't you?" I replied and everyone around us laughed, even though it was a very serious question.

"Come and get something to eat. You didn't win, by the way."

I looked over to the bonfire where the Mountain Maulers were jumping onto each other's backs and passing around a giant golden trophy. "Shame. I thought we stood a real chance," I said scanning the group, trying to see in the dim light just who I was hanging out with. I spotted Amelie, who threw her arms around me. Once she pulled away I saw her face harden as she glared at Tawny and Talia. The Ts recoiled a little under Amelie's stern gaze.

"Oh, it's okay. We're friends now," I reassured my cousin, and she instantly melted into an easy smile.

"Great, I'm Amelie, Tig's cousin."

Thirty-two

It was strange. Two weeks had passed at Alpine Adventure, and here on the last night they were finally getting to meet each other. Maddie and Aurelia from the yellow team brought us Ts three plates of warm crusty, buttery bread and three mugs of steamy soup and we all nestled into a huddle on the floor, exchanging stories and mountainside adventures. Some drama kid with a similar mane of orange hair told Tawny about the history of drama, while two girls and Talia shared their mutual love of world literature. I told everyone about our big falling out and how Tawny slipped off the bridge, and everyone laughed. No one was judging me or the Ts, and we weren't judging them. I was too tired to try and fit in anyway, and to my surprise I didn't really have to.

It was all going so well, until a familiar voice cut across our happy circle. "Ah, Tiggy Tig Tig, I thought the plan was to lose them on the mountain? I guess you couldn't shake off the 'Ts' in the end?" Kim stood over our huddle, the glow of the fire lighting up one side of his face, while a long shadow fell across the other.

My mind crumbled into a million pieces as I tried to think of a fast response, something witty or clever, something to bring Kim down and prove to everyone that my loyalty was with Talia and Tawny. This was the guy who had hijacked my YouTube channel, destroyed my friendship with the Ts and . . . the thought of Fidge came back into my mind and I knew witty or funny wouldn't be enough. It was time to speak some hard truth: "Kim, you have hurt a lot of people, and you had no right to go on my phone and edit my videos. The pain you have caused . . ."

Kim snorted as he imitated my voice. "The pain you have caused. Tiggy Tig Tig, you're so dramatic."

I pushed through. "Maybe I am. But you don't know that, because you don't know me."

"Everyone knows you. You throw your life all over YouTube."

I swallowed down my pride and took another deep breath. "You don't know Tawny or Talia or Fidge. And I don't know enough about you to care about what you think of me either."

An awkward silence hovered around the group as Kim shuffled anxiously on his feet. "Come on, Tiggy Tig Tig, we know each other. What about all those lunch dates? You couldn't wait to bring me all the little cakes and treats."

My stomach rolled over. He was relentless. I scrapped around for some words, but every time I thought I had a closing statement that would make him leave, Kim had the power to twist it back round to another conversation.

"They were not dates, and I don't want to talk to you any more," I said. Kim was smiling, his confidence was unshakable.

"Okay, we are done here!" Ismene jumped to her feet and stood in front of Kim. Kim smiled – he seemed delighted to have some new attention from my sister and I wanted so much for Ismene to sit down and be quiet, but she continued: "You can go now, Kim. We aren't interested in hearing what you have to say."

Kim glared into my sister's eyes, his pop-star smile glowing even in the darkness. "Ismene, interesting. So Tiggy isn't the only fiery Kingsley sister after all."

"Yes, very perceptive of you. Goodbye."

In a move I have never seen Ismene make, she put her arms on Kim's shoulders, twisted him around and sent him on his merry way. And Kim obeyed. He just walked away.

We all sat for a moment in silence, Amelie and I trying to fit this new bold Kim-crushing Ismene with the timid brainiac we knew and loved. Through the silence I heard Tawny's squeaky voice whisper out, "Tiggy Tig Tig, your sister is so cool!"

Thirty-three

My bags were packed and our dorm room was empty. Talia, Tawny and I stood in the art room peering down at the little tree. Jada stood opposite us looking at the sculpture from a different angle. "I like it. You would never think you were a beginner, Antigone." I smiled, still not sure if I loved it too, but happy enough.

"Well, Miss Tanner is extraordinary. She has taught very many beginners, Tiggy Tig Tig. I told you she was an inspiration." Talia spoke with passion and sincerity, which I had come to find both amusing and loveable in her.

"You did tell me that, Talia, very many times."

Tawny reached out a hand and tapped the squatty, scruffy owl at the end. "This one is beautiful – she looks so sweet. Can you make me one?"

It was a good question. Could I make it again? Did I even want to? "Maybe, but I think I need some more practice before I start giving my work out as gifts." It was the oddest sensation to have all of those eyes scrutinizing my work. Looking at it closely and finding meaning in its imperfection. It wasn't that good, it wasn't even close, but I didn't really mind. There was something about the tree that felt like balance – like nothing was perfect but everything was okay; it felt like it had harmony . . . that was the challenge, right?

Miss Tanner came out of her little office with a cardboard box in her hand. "This should be big enough for your sculpture but small enough for hand luggage, Antigone." She placed the box on the desk next to my tree.

"Okay, girls, time to go. Bring it in for a hug." Jada stretched out her arms and gave us a group squeeze. Our first meeting felt like a million worlds ago and those first impressions of Miss Tanner, the Ts, everything about Alpine Adventure, seemed so different to the people standing around me now. As much as I wanted to go home – needed to go home – I knew I was going to miss Alpine too.

Miss Tanner began packing the sculpture carefully into the box.

Jada pulled out my phone from her pocket. "Here you are, Antigone, your phone!"

I looked at it briefly, not sure whether having it back was going to bring relief or more bad news. I nodded my thanks and stuffed it into my coat pocket. Jada gave us all one more hug before leaving us in the studio.

I turned to Talia and Tawny, already knowing they had people waiting for them.

Tawny was filled with wide-eyed hope as she asked, "Are you going to come back next year, Tiggy?"

I hated to disappoint her, but who knew what Auntie Kate would decide to do with me next! "I hope so. I am going to really try."

"Good," said Talia. "I am going to add you to the Ts' WhatsApp group and next year we must request a room with four beds, because Teresa will be back for sure, and she really can't wait to meet you, Tiggy Tig Tig." She was taking notes down as she spoke, already building the itinerary for next year.

I looked at my two new friends, busying themselves to include me, enjoying my imperfect work and giving me all the love I needed. How had that ever not been enough? Without thinking, I threw my arms around them both and planted a big kiss in the middle of Tawny's bright orange hair. "You girls are the greatest. I am going to call you all the time."

Talia squeezed her hand out from under the cuddle to add another note. "Oh yes, you must always call us, Tiggy, every single day."

"Oh, I will, very many times." I released them both from my enthusiastic hug. It was time to go. In just a few minutes I would be on a coach, driving away from Alpine Adventure, not knowing if I would ever return.

Noticing our reluctance to leave each other, Miss Tanner began to usher us out. "Come on, girls. School starts next week; it's time to get ready for the new term."

I headed out of the room with Talia and Tawny, secretly wishing I could have given Miss Tanner a hug too.

Just as the door was about to close behind me, Miss Tanner called me back in. "Antigone, aren't you forgetting something?" She held out the box with my sculpture neatly wrapped inside.

I ran back in and took it from her. "Thank you, Miss Tanner, and thank you for everything."

Miss Tanner smiled warmly at me. "Have a safe flight, Tiggy Tig Tig."

I left the art studio for the final time and as the door clicked firmly closed behind me, I cuddled a little tighter to the cardboard box that held my latest piece of work. On top I noticed a label. Miss Tanner must have put it on when she wrapped it up. I flipped it over to read what she had written.

Three Ts sitting in a Tree
by Antigone Kingsley

Epilogue

. . . And so, notebook, here I am, back on a flight to Paris. I have conquered the great unknown of Geneva. I overcame the Swiss Alps, found new friends and even escaped the charms of K-pop Kim. I guess I can overcome a lot of things. . .

I pull my phone out of my pocket and turn it around again and again in my hand. I haven't turned it on since that horrible moment when I threw it across the dorm room. I can't turn it on now that the plane is in mid-air. Then we will land and the whole family will be around. My heart starts to accelerate as the bitter taste of dread fills my mouth. How will I be able to repair things on the phone? Should I wait until I get back?

. . . I think Fidge may hate me. I think he might think I hate him. I don't. Not at all. Not even close. . .

My hand trembles as I try to keep the pen steady on the page. It was much easier to put Fidge in a box to deal with later when there were so many other things around to distract me. I close my eyes as a whole army of accusations floods my mind. I should never have trusted Kim. I should have told Fidge the truth, that Kim was not a girl and that he hated the Ts. I should have stayed quiet and not tried to make friends with everyone. I should delete my dumb YouTube channel.

I force my eyes open and shake the assault out of my mind.

I can't go back in time, as much as I wish I could. So I have to keep moving forward. I have to face my family and I have to face Auntie Kate. And I have to face Fidge. I have *to tell him the truth. All of it.*

I look at my phone. Powerless and yet holding a thousand mysteries. I have overcome a lot without it. I pick it up and feel its weight grow in my hand, heavier and hotter all at once. I look for a place to keep it safe but far away from me. Amelie and Ismene are both fast asleep, so I stuff it into the side pocket of Amelie's bag. It is time to face my biggest challenge of all. There cannot be any distractions.

Notebook, I am going to speak with Fidge, face to face. Not on the phone but in real life. I am going to look him straight in the eye and use every ounce of strength I have within me to make it all okay again. Better than okay. I know I can do this. Because I am Antigone Kingsley, YouTube sensation, reformed attempted murderer and Alpine Adventurer. But more than that, I am Antigone Kingsley, Fidge's very best friend, and I WILL fix this.

Coming in 2025 . . .

Antigone Kingsley: Masquerade

Acknowledgements

Here we are again at the end of another tempestuous time with Tig, and it wouldn't be complete without sending out a few thank yous!

First and foremost, special thanks to Deborah Lock and the whole team at SPCK for bringing Antigone back for another adventure.

I am hugely grateful to Tony, Ana, Alvaro, and Blanca for hosting our Swiss research trip together, and to Lilia and Blanca, who created the wonderful Miss Tanner over that same weekend! I hope she is everything you imagined and more.

I am so grateful to the students at Imaginarium Academy for their ongoing support and ideas in relation to Tig, and in particular Twyla, Chloe, Matilda, Marnie, Lolly, Joshua, Ana, Blanca, Lilia, Lucrezia, Dan, and Edie for their work in bringing Antigone's first book to the London National Youth Theatre Stage. You guys brought so much colour to these characters, and I LOVED all of your contributions!

Thank you to Mum, Dad, and the sisters for being easy sounding boards, big encouragers, and super chilled when I forget your birthdays (which is always when I am busy writing . . . or doing anything for that matter!).

Dominic, thank you, thank you, THANK YOU for being the biggest cheerleader, for creating space for us all to follow our imagination, and for always finding ways to make our dreams come true.

Finally, thank you Lilia and Reuben for being beautiful, adventurous, loving, fun, and brilliant kids. You both inspire me every day, and I am incredibly grateful to call you mine. Go Team ;-)

A perfect coming-of-age companion for girls aged 10 plus going through the highs and lows of growing up

9781910674697 • £8.99

Paperback • 256 Pages

AVAILABLE NOW

spck group

TiG
xoxo